Death

A
Percy
Pontefract
Cozy Mystery

AT A

Christmas
Party

ANN SUTTON

Death

at a

Christmas

Party

By

Ann Sutton

A merry Christmas party with old friends. A dead body in the kitchen. A reluctant heroine. Sounds like a recipe for a jolly festive murder mystery!

It is 1928 and a group of old friends gather for their annual Christmas party. The food, drink and goodwill flow, and everyone has a rollicking good time.

When the call of nature forces the accident-prone Percy Pontefract up, in the middle of the night, she realizes she is in need of a little midnight snack and wanders into the kitchen. But she gets more than she bargained for when she trips over a dead body.

Ordered to remain in the house by the grumpy inspector sent to investigate the case, Percy stumbles upon facts about her friends that shake her to the core and cause her to suspect more than one of them of the dastardly deed.

Finally permitted to go home, Percy tells her trusty cook all the awful details. Rather than sympathize, the cook encourages her to do some investigating of her own. After all, who knows these people better than Percy? Reluctant at first, Percy begins poking into her friends' lives, discovering they all harbor dark secrets. However, none seem connected to the murder…at first glance.

Will Percy put herself and her children in danger before she can solve the case that has the police stumped?

A totally gripping historical whodunnit introducing a charming, delightfully flawed, new, female sleuth.

Death at a Christmas Party is Book 1 in the new Percy Pontefract Historical Cozy Mystery Series.

Published by

Wild Poppy Publishing LLC
Highland, UT 84003

Distributed by Wild Poppy Publishing

Cover design by Julie Matern
Cover Design ©2022 Wild Poppy Publishing LLC

Edited by Jolene Perry

Dedicated to Mary Kersey, my Mum, who passed away before she could read any of my books.

Style Note

I am a naturalized American citizen born and raised in the United Kingdom. I have readers in America, the UK, Australia, Canada and beyond. But my book is set in the United Kingdom.

So which version of English should I choose?

I chose American English as it is my biggest audience, my family learns this English and my editor suggested it was the most logical.

This leads to criticism from those in other English-speaking countries, but I have neither the time nor the resources to do a special edition for each country.

I do use British words, phrases and idioms whenever I can (unless my editor does not understand them and then it behooves me to change it so that it is not confusing to my readers).

Table of Contents

Chapter 1
England
1928

Persephone Pontefract eyed the narrow stairs.

Mortifying memories of Aunt Euphemia's funeral fiasco sprouted like thorny weeds. She looked down at her size twelve foot and gauged the first step. Her broad mouth pulled down into an unattractive shrug that would have been sure to garner a criticism from her mother, had she been in attendance. But there was no getting out of this. She was the last speaker at the St. Wilfred's Academy for Boys, Christmas prayer service, and in order to attain the lectern, the portable steps had to be navigated.

Glancing to the side, she saw William send her an encouraging lop-sided smile. *Dear boy.* She drew in a deep, steadying breath but let it out quickly as the middle button on her jacket strained against her ample chest. It would likely take out the headmaster's eye if it popped off. Settling her shoulders, she straightened her red, felt hat.

Striding purposefully toward the dais, Percy placed her right foot firmly onto the first step. As she had calculated, it was not wide enough to accommodate her whole foot and she wobbled as the other one hovered in mid-air. Feeling her center of gravity shift, she flung out her hands, the red, leather handbag swinging violently, as her arms became human windmills.

Gasps peppered the room as she attempted to gain traction by forcing her left foot onto the next step, however, only her toe made contact with the wood and in a puff of red tartan, she fell backward into the lap of Mr. Montague, knocking him over in his chair so that they both fell to the ground at the feet of Miss Trowbridge, the music teacher.

1

Staring straight up, cushioned by Mr. Montague, Percy had a clear view of thick petticoats and a hairy chin.

The mathematics teacher pushed her up, spluttering about cracked glasses as Percy gathered the shreds of her dignity around her, like the worn battle flag of a defeated army, amidst the buzz of whispering parents.

She dared not look at William for fear of the shame she might see etched on his innocent, freckled face.

If only I could make it through one day without embarrassing myself, or my children.

Swallowing down a sob of humiliation, Percy leapt back up the three stairs, landing badly and rolling her ankle as she lurched for the lectern.

"Good afternoon," she panted, clutching the podium and looking out over the crowd of amused students and parents. Her mind went completely blank. She blinked several times willing her mind to engage until she spotted little William pointing to her bag. *Ah yes! My speech!*

Unclipping the large, brass clasp of her handbag, she dug into the copious interior, triumphantly holding the folded paper aloft. William smiled and gave his mother a thumbs-up as the overwrought audience sighed in unison.

Pursing frosted-pink lips over large, front teeth, she drew a hand across the crumpled paper.

"Headmaster. Parents. Students. As the Secretary of the St. Wilfred's board of governors, I wish you all a merry Christmas." A smattering of applause followed.

"Christmas is a time to look around and think of those less fortunate than ourselves. I am happy to report that this year's Harvest Fair raised £100 which will be donated to St. Mary's Orphanage. Your generosity will buy gifts for the children who will spend Christmas without a family."

Another ripple of applause.

She meandered through the rest of her short speech with no further catastrophes and set her eyes on the safety of her seat. However, as she turned to vacate the lectern, her heel caught the wooden stand's edge and, spinning uncontrollably, she fell from the dais into a large, decorated Christmas tree. *Snap!*

Instantly, the headmaster jumped down to rescue Percy by pulling on her arms, but alas, he was unable to spring her five feet eleven frame from the giant pot. Only with assistance from the deputy head did they succeed in freeing her, as the congregation sang a rousing carol, but not before a blinding camera flash.

Great! National infamy as well as public humiliation.

Percy stood, black spots before her eyes, brushing soil from her suit while trying to regain her balance and stagger back to her seat in the front row.

After the benediction, the crowd began to buzz and move, eager to begin their Christmas holidays. Percy sat still, her gaze lingering on the murdered tree.

"Mummy!" cried William, coming to claim her. Bartholomew, however, was nowhere to be seen. She imagined his pale, pre-adolescent face, glowing like the poinsettias around them. "Your speech was very good," continued William. "Did Daddy help you write it?"

"No, he did not! I may be clumsy, but I am perfectly capable of writing a decent speech." The words came out with more force than she intended. Upon seeing the hurt in her younger son's eyes, she changed her tone and kissed his cheek. "But I am flattered that you think it as good as one of Daddy's." She had not seen her eight-year-old son since half term and crushed him into a bear hug.

"Mummy," he protested. "I'm too big for that now."

Her heart cracked.

She really hated the barbaric tradition of boarding school. What other civilized nation evicted their young from the family home at the tender age of eight to be raised by strangers in drafty castles?

3

When Bartholomew had left for St. Wilfred's three years ago, he had taken half her heart with him. William's departure had taken the rest.

For the first time since she had become a mother, she now rattled around their rambling country home alone. Well, not alone exactly. She still had her husband Piers when he wasn't traveling for work, Apollo, their ancient chocolate Labrador, and the beloved cook, Mrs. Appleby.

She glanced around the assembly hall, watching the petite, slender mothers dressed in the latest fashions, wearing hats that cost more than most people earned in a year, as they scooped up their young to take them home for the winter break. Her sight settled on Lilly Lawrence, a friend from her own school days whom she met at Kew Gardens for the annual flower show. Catching Percy's eye, Lilly weaved her way through the crowd.

"Thought you were going to crop it," said Lilly chuckling. "It reminded me of—"

"Yes, well," said Percy, interrupting her before she shared yet another awkward moment from Percy's recent past. "Let's not go into that now."

"Do you hurt anywhere?" asked Lilly.

Percy was aware of several tender spots sprouting, and her ankle was throbbing angrily. "No. I'm fine." She caught a glimpse of eleven-year-old Bartholomew hiding behind a pillar in the back of the room.

"How did you fill your time with both boys at school?" asked Lilly. "I hired a professional tennis coach and joined the golf club."

Percy looked down at her impossibly long legs. "Can you really see me playing tennis?" she asked.

"Point taken. So, what *did* you do?" Lilly was aging well and bore no scars from bearing three children.

"I visited mother too often and ate cake," replied Percy pulling on the tight waistband of her skirt.

4

"Ah," said Lilly, examining Percy's expansive girth. "How about trying golf? I can sponsor you for the club, if you'd like."

"I'm having a vision," said Percy with a wry smile. "Instead of the ball sailing toward the hole, the club is swinging through the air to kill some poor unsuspecting passerby."

"Yes, you're probably right," agreed Lilly. "Sport is not really your thing. Perhaps you could join an amateur dramatics society or take up poetry reading."

Percy wrinkled her large nose. "Anything is better than the eternal corridor of nothingness I was in last term, I suppose."

The hall had mostly emptied out and Bartholomew finally appeared from behind the pillar, his bottom lip jutting out, his young brow knitted. Her heart cramped.

"At least we can enjoy the boys over Christmas," said Lilly, heading for the doors. "Happy Christmas, Percy."

Now that the hall was completely empty, Bartholomew approached her. "Quick, let's go before anyone sees us together."

Merry Christmas to you, too!

Chapter 2

Breakfast in the Pontefract house was a rather informal affair when Percy's husband was away on business. Hearty food eaten in the cozy kitchen. But when Piers Pontefract was home, they ate in the dining room on the second-best china, her husband insisting that the boys be down and dressed by eight o'clock when they were not at school.

Today they were in the dining room. Piers had made it home after midnight and though he tried to be quiet, had woken her. Percy's head felt fuzzy from interrupted sleep, and the bruises that had begun yesterday were in purple, painful bloom this morning.

"Um, I shall be gone for the next two days," Piers informed her as he scanned the morning paper while the boys made train noises.

"What!" cried Percy. "But it's the Howard's annual Christmas party tonight. You can't miss it."

He squinted at her over the top of black-rimmed reading glasses. "I can and I must. I am in the service of her majesty's government and when they call, I respond."

Percy slammed her cheek onto her palm in resignation. "I suppose I shall just stay home then."

"Why?" asked her husband with a frown. "Boys, keep it down please."

"What do you mean, why?" She tapped her finger on the cloth above William's plate to indicate that he should eat.

"Mrs. Appleby will be here to watch the boys, and you deserve a night out."

"I do?"

"Certainly. Just because I can't be there shouldn't mean you have to sit at home all glum." His widely spaced eyes creased into what might be described as a frown but having been married to the man for over twelve years, Percy knew it to be a smile. "Go and have a jolly good time."

"Alright then!" she declared, confiscating a pen knife that was being used to make holes in the tablecloth. "Where are you going?"

"Oh, here and there." It was the same answer Piers gave whenever she asked.

Percy had taken the boys riding after their father left for work. They did not own horses but were members of a local riding club a few miles from home. It was a beloved activity that was always sure to knock them out. Even now, they were curled up by the fire with their tin soldiers, eyelids heavy. They would be fast asleep before she left for the Howard's.

She checked her bumpy appearance in the mirror over the fireplace and adjusted the shoulders of her red Christmas dress. It was over ten years old but was one of her favorites and only worn a couple of times a year. As she ran a hand over her bulging stomach, she encountered a moth hole. *No-one will notice.* She ran a ring finger over the pink lipstick. Did it matter that she wore pink lips with a red dress? She squinted her eyes and shook her head. It was fine.

Leaning down to kiss the top of each boy's head, she felt a couple of stitches pop. Bartholomew barely moved but William gave her a sleepy smile. "You smell like flowers."

"Thank you. Now, be good fellows for Mrs. Appleby and go to bed exactly when she tells you."

She checked her little clutch for lipstick and face powder and grabbed the overnight bag by the door as the taxi honked its horn. Throwing her old, fur-rimmed coat on, she hurried out the door into the crisp, cold night. Catching sight of the cozy picture of her boys by the fire, she toyed briefly with the idea of canceling her plans.

"Hampstead," she told the driver, and the car crunched out of the driveway and pulled them onto the country road that would take them into the city.

Due to a downpour of heavy rain, Percy was more than fashionably late, which meant that everyone else was already there by the time she arrived. The Howard's were some of their oldest friends and Thomas Howard had served alongside Piers in the war.

"Percy, darling," said Verity Howard with her honking voice. "No Piers? I thought you might have changed your mind." She examined Percy's face and pointed a finger at her. "You almost did, didn't you?" The pitch and decibel level indicated that Verity had already imbibed at least three cocktails.

"Only for a second," admitted Percy. "The boys have only just got home, and I've missed them terribly."

"I give you three days before you're wishing them back at school," cackled Verity. "My two are already bickering. They're at mother's for the night." She clapped her hands in the middle of the Edwardian drawing room, its walls and shelves festooned with fir branches, candles and holly. It reminded Percy that she should get out her own decorations.

"Now that Percy is finally here, we can go in to dinner."

All the men had been at school together and the wives had been added over the years. They had been meeting together for the Howard's Christmas party every year, except during the Great War. Percy had first come as a new fiancée and been welcomed by the crowd.

Verity and Tom led the way across the hall to the vaulted dining room where an enormous Christmas tree stood in the large bow window. A variety of glossy nutcrackers lined the ornate fireplace. Percy followed the Goodfellows, Jemima and Bruce. Still handsome, Bruce usually ended the evening sloshed, which embarrassed quiet Jemima no end. Behind them were the Richmonds, Ellen and Mark. Their star had risen after Mark made a fortunate investment that had quickly tripled in value. They claimed the influx of wealth had not changed them, but it had. And lastly, the Valentines, Phoebe and Walter. Walter had lost a leg at the Somme and winced when he walked.

Jolly green and red napkins awaited them at each place, along with a shiny Christmas cracker. They always waited until dessert to pull them.

Tom stood at the head of the table, holding up his Waterford crystal goblet.

"May I say how good it is to be together again—— though we miss Piers." He nodded in Percy's direction. "I'm beyond grateful that we have been able to preserve this tradition for so many years. Let us toast to continuing it for many more! Cheers!"

"Hear! Hear!" cried everyone around the table holding their own glasses high and clinking them with their neighbors.

A maid brought in a handsome goose and laid it before Tom who theatrically brandished the carving knife while sharpening it. The room filled with the comforting smell of the bird and the fragrant mashed potatoes.

Percy relaxed.

"Our grateful thanks to Mrs. Barlow, for providing such a smashing feast," declared Tom, as the Howard's cook, dressed in a charcoal dress and spotless apron, slipped into the room for a second and bowed her gray head. Everybody applauded as the color rose on the cook's wrinkled cheek. She removed a dainty handkerchief and wiped her bulbous nose before retreating with a pleasant smile.

"Where is old Piers then?" asked Walter as Tom handed round the platter.

"Away on business," she replied while tucking into her goose. She did appreciate good food.

"Ah!" said Walter, tapping his nose and winking.

It wasn't just Verity who had over-imbibed it would seem. Percy's forehead creased, she offered him a half-smile, and went back to her food.

"We've just returned from the most glorious cruise around the French Riviera," said Ellen to the table in general. The only holidays Percy's family could manage were day trips to Brighton and a couple of weeks in Devon.

"How marvelous!" gushed Jemima. "I've always wanted to do that, haven't I, Bruce?"

"She has, but I can't stand the garlic myself. Use too much of it, in my opinion."

Percy bit her cheek. *Who would pass up a trip to the Riviera because they didn't like garlic?* Perhaps he had seen more of France than he ever wanted to in the war, and this was a convenient excuse to avoid traveling there.

"We went to Jersey with my parents in September," remarked Phoebe, fingering a pretty ruby necklace. "Daddy managed to get time off from his job in government, finally. We were blessed with an Indian summer. It was glorious."

"Isn't it hard to be away from your business for so long?" Tom asked Mark, regarding the cruise.

"I've hired an assistant, a man I trust with my life," he responded. "He takes care of everything while I'm away."

"The donkeys were very lively in Devon this summer," blurted out Percy. Everyone in the room stopped eating and stared at her. "The locals were very pleased at the amount of manure they produced."

With red lips tightly puckered, Verity responded. "Percy! I hardly think that's appropriate dinner talk." A giggle dribbled out like drops from an over filled glass.

Percy put a palm to her hot cheek. "Oh, yes. I suppose so." She tried to laugh off her faux pas but the sound was more like a strangled cat. She stared at her plate.

The conversation resumed, the topics ranging from home repairs, to children, to the state of the world. Percy kept her head down and asked for seconds of everything to keep her unreliable mouth busy.

"Time for crackers!" announced Tom as the dinner plates were removed.

Since Piers was not in attendance, Percy held the cracker loosely, trying to catch someone's eye. Loud snaps split the air around the room as crackers exploded, shooting forth trinkets, riddles and colorful paper crowns. Laughing heartily, the guests unfolded the hats and read the riddles.

"Percy!" yelled tipsy Tom. "Where's your hat?"

She waved her lonely cracker.

"Walter! Pull her cracker!" he demanded.

Walter stood and reached across the table, yanking the cracker clear out of Percy's hand sending him into a fit of laughter. "Try again." He offered her the cracker and Percy got a good grip. This time she got the better of him and he fell forward into the gravy bowl, but the cracker did not burst open.

"Oops."

A drip of the tasty plum sauce hung from Walter's sleeve and he popped it into his mouth.

"Third time's a charm," he sang, clearly well lubed with alcohol.

This time they both pulled equally hard and the satisfying *crack* rang out to universal cheers. A silver keyring landed in Percy's goblet.

As she unfolded the hat to place it over her carefully sculpted hair, hoping it would not undo her hard work, the maid returned with the blazing Christmas pudding, doused liberally with brandy. Everybody cheered again as the electric lights were turned off and the blue and orange flames licked the sides of the enormous pudding.

"Is there a sixpence?" shouted Jemima.

"Of course!" cried Verity. "It's not a proper Christmas pudding without one!"

Percy's eyes widened with pleasure as generous portions were passed around with a jug full of rich brandy sauce. She would indulge tonight and watch her portions tomorrow.

The wine was working its way into her blood stream and she could feel her joints and inhibitions loosen up. On the third bite her teeth hit something hard.

"I got it!" she cried, holding the dirty sixpence up high. "Good luck for me next year!"

Someone began to sing a rollicking carol, and they all joined in sounding more like hooligans at a football match than mature adults.

After dessert, and cheese and biscuits, they eventually made their way back to the drawing room for the traditional games. Percy caught a glimpse of herself in the mirror over the fireplace; her wiry, wild hair was beginning to crumble, and her hat was more than a little askew. They always played charades and 'Guess that Tune' around the piano. Charades was not Percy's forte and she hoped that since she was alone she would be spared from having to mime.

They started around the antique grand piano with Verity playing the first few notes of a song and the rest having to guess the title. Percy was usually pretty good, but she was having trouble making her mouth obey her brain as she drank her second glass of rummy eggnog.

By the time they sat for charades, she felt very merry and more than a little sleepy. Glancing at the clock she saw it was well after midnight and wondered vaguely where Piers was tonight.

Bruce, a civil servant like her husband, interrupted her musings with his turn at charades. As he held the paper to read his task, diamond cufflinks glittered in the low light, then he was flinging his tall frame around the room, palms together, opening his arms like a giant mouth, chasing his diminutive wife.

"Moby Dick!" cried Mark.

"Got it!" Bruce responded, flopping heavily into a comfy armchair, his sharp jaw flushed from the exertion.

The amusing game continued until only Percy had not participated.

"Your turn, lovely!" said Verity.

"Do I have to since I don't have Piers?"

"Absolutely! It's tradition!"

Percy pushed herself out of the deep sofa and felt her head spin for just a moment. She put out a steadying hand. Looking down at her enormous feet, she concentrated on walking in a straight line to Verity as everyone laughed and cajoled around her.

Reaching for the slip of paper in Verity's hand, she stumbled on the rug and grasped the mantle, sending a spray of fir branches tumbling off and toppling a tall nutcracker. No one seemed to notice.

She looked at the paper.

The Marriage of Figaro.

She indicated how many words were needed and that it was an opera and decided to plump for the partial word 'fig'. Lifting her hand as if to pluck fruit from a tree she pulled and then inspected the phantom fruit in her hand.

"Apple!"

"Pear! Partridge in a pear tree!"

"Plum!"

She shook her head and saw the thin paper hat float to her feet.

Deciding to try a different word she smoothed her hands over her head and down her shoulders to her waist.

"Lady Godiva!"

She rolled her eyes with a giggle and held her hands as if holding a bouquet.

"Praying!"

"Hoping!"

"Pain!"

She kept her hands together and walked slowly as if down the aisle.

"Funeral!" shouted Mark as she caught her foot on the fireplace edge and fell flat on her face.

The whole room erupted into raucous laughter. Percy felt no pain and rolled onto her back, shaking with mirth.

It wasn't a terrible way to end the night.

Chapter 3

Percy woke up to pitch black, her bladder screaming, her head throbbing.

She felt the bed for Piers. He was not there which wasn't unusual. As she sniffed lemon furniture polish and felt damask beneath her fingers it took another minute to remember where she was. *The Howards.*

Grabbing her fluffy robe, she shoved both feet into her masculine slippers and headed for the door. As she stepped into the hall, she heard a bird. *Wait! At this time of night?* Perhaps it was a giggle. The landing was partially lit by a crescent moon as she padded across the thick rug. A creak stopped her mid step. Silence. The house was at least a hundred years old, and it squeaked and wheezed like an old lady. She increased her speed. Another wooden groan seemed to come from the stairs, but she was too far along to see who it was. Imagining a rush on the lavatory she picked up her speed. Thankfully, when she tried the handle, no one else was using the facilities and she slipped in as the grandfather clock in the vestibule struck three. Closing the door, she pulled the cord for the overhead light. The instant glare assaulted her pupils. She quickly snapped it off again as her retinas burned the image of the toilet into her brain.

After pulling the chain, the plumbing made loud, guttural sounds like the bowels of a hibernating dragon. She flinched, hoping she wouldn't wake the household.

Her bladder now at peace, her tummy began to grumble in competition with the cistern. What was the harm in going to the kitchen in search of a light snack since she was up?

The smooth soles of her slippers glided along the thick Persian rug like blades on ice and she only resisted the juvenile urge to slide down the curved, oak banister

15

because of the banging of her head. *I would just end up in a heap at the bottom anyway and wake everyone up, for sure.*

Gripping the handrail tightly, she pattered down the stairs. Halfway, she halted at the sound of a *click*. She knew that noise. It was a bedroom door closing in the upper hallway. Straining her ears, she hesitated. *Would she appear to be a glutton if discovered?* However, when no one appeared after several seconds, she hurried along the dark hall to the empty kitchen. The lingering scent of last night's feast still hung in the air and her stomach progressed from grumbling to growling.

A half curtain at the kitchen window allowed the moonlight in and since her eyes had more than adjusted, she refrained from turning on the light. No need to advertise her scavenging. The white icebox shone, beckoning to her like a siren and she tiptoed over to answer its call.

Milk and cheese sat awaiting her and she took each one out, tenderly placing them on the hardy, wooden table. Reaching back in for the cold carcass sitting in a dish, her mouth watered.

"A late-night meal fit for a king," she whispered to herself.

Running her hand along the counter she found a bread bin containing half a cottage loaf. Fortunately, the bread knife was tucked into the edge of the bin. Withdrawing both she installed her generous bottom on the bench by the table.

After two healthy portions of thickly sliced bread and farmer's cheddar, she gulped back milk straight from the bottle. She could almost hear her mother berating her. She didn't care. There was no one to see and what they didn't know wouldn't hurt them.

Wiping her mouth with the back of her hand instead of using a napkin, she turned her attention to the meat, holding it to her nose and sniffing. *Mmm. Cold goose.*

16

She ran a finger around the plate to scoop up the congealed meat jelly then popped it into her mouth where it melted against her tongue. *Heaven!* Carefully pulling the flesh from the bone with two fingers, she pushed the tender meat into her mouth. Perhaps goose was her favorite. She went back for seconds until her thirst demanded more milk.

What she really needed now, to top everything off, was something sweet. *Christmas pudding!* Pushing back from the table, the bench squealed like a stuck pig. Heart in her throat, she froze again.

Several seconds passed in profound silence. No one had stirred. She swung her legs up and over the bench and ventured back to the counter where she had found the bread. Searching the other end, she saw a large plate with a bowl upside down. *Bingo!*

It was at clandestine moments like this where she was most likely to drop things. She rubbed her greasy hands on her robe and carefully gripped the sides of the ceramic bowl. It slipped. She gasped but caught it and replacing the bowl, cleaned her hands once more. The second time she was successful. Before her was the brown treasure she sought. She tipped the bowl the right way up and placed it next to the pudding, nudging the pot of brandy sauce in the process. *Perfect!*

Now to find a plate.

Opening the upper cupboard, she found a tea set and removed a saucer. *Knife.* She padded back to retrieve the bread knife, cut a healthy slice of the fruity concoction, then drowned it in thick, cold brandy sauce. Her eyes bulged in anticipation. *Spoon.*

This proved harder to find and she was into her fourth drawer before succeeding. Grabbing the spoon and the overflowing saucer, she slid back onto the bench and plunged the utensil into the sugary dessert. Closing her eyes in sheer ecstasy, she let the nostalgic mixture sit on her tongue and perform its magic. The lovely taste evoked memories from Christmases past and a vision of Granny Crabtree swam into her mind, squeezing her heart with the memory.

Granny had been gone more than ten years. At six feet even, she was the only one who truly understood Percy and the feminine difficulties of maneuvering excessive height. She tapped the spoon on her bottom teeth and sighed.

Mouthful after mouthful brought more and more memories of her father's mother, and she happily reminisced. If only her own mother were half as understanding. She had been nothing but embarrassed by Percy's size since the day she was born and cringed whenever Percy stumbled.

Percy scraped the saucer thoroughly, then throwing manners to the wind, picked up the china plate and licked it clean. The thought of further scandalizing her mother brought a smile to her face. She toyed with the idea of another helping but thought better of it and padded over to the sink to leave her dirty things there for the staff to clean the next morning.

She cautiously replaced the bowl over the pudding, returned the milk and meat to the icebox, and bread to its bin, without incident. *Almost on the homestretch.* She had left two bones on the table and picked them up to take to the dustbin which she knew was hidden in the large pantry larder.

That corner of the kitchen was much darker and as she pulled open the door to the windowless room, it reminded her of waking up to the pitch darkness. She felt for the string to turn on the light but could not find it. Stepping in to the dark, her foot hit a soft object and she felt herself pitching forward. Propelling her arms back did little to stop the forward momentum and she continued her forward flight, bracing for the hard floor. Instead, she landed on something squishy that broke her fall. Rolling off she opened her eyes, finding herself nose to nose with a cold, hard eyeball.

Percy promptly lost the contents of her stomach.

Chapter 4

The whole house was in a total uproar.

Percy sat trembling on the settee wrapped in a tartan, scratchy wool blanket, her stomach still doing somersaults, holding a gigantic mug of sickly-sweet tea. Policeman in big black boots and the other inhabitants of the house, were walking back and forth in a whirlwind and talking at her periodically, but she could not focus on any of it.

She had fallen onto a dead woman.

In the pantry.

She shivered.

Percy had learned that the deceased was none other than the Howard's cook, Mrs. Barlow, and that she had been hit over the head with a blunt object. *What kind of speak was that? Blunt object?* She shivered again.

Verity squatted down in front of Percy and patted her hand.

"How are you feeling, Percy dear?" she honked. "You've had quite a shock. Can I call Piers for you?"

Percy's jaw sagged as her drooping lids lifted. "I don't know where he is." She felt her eyes stinging.

"How about calling home, then?"

"No!" She didn't mean to shout but she did not want the boys to hear about this. "Sorry, I just don't want them to know. William and Bartie are being taken care of, blissfully unaware of this drama and I am among friends. I just need the shock to wear off." A small pulse began to beat in her eye lid.

"What were you doing up at that time of night?" asked Verity, moving to sit beside her on the settee.

"I—I had to use the loo and then realized I was a bit hungry," she stammered. "I'm familiar with the layout of your kitchen so thought I would snoop around for some leftovers. I was just putting a couple of bones in the bin when—" She swallowed down a sob.

"There, there." Verity put an arm around her. "The inspector would like a word with everyone. Do you think you could manage that?"

This was the very last thing Percy felt she could manage but she nodded.

"Then I shall take you to Tom's office."

Verity tried to lift Percy but she was too heavy, so Percy struggled to her feet with one arm, trying not to slosh hot tea everywhere. She was still dressed in her thick, flannel nightdress, fluffy robe and slippers, but the blanket was a comfort and it was slipping.

"Here you are, Inspector," announced Verity and pushed Percy into the room.

A solemn, heavy man sat on the other side of Tom's desk. His stern face split into a false smile. "Mrs. Pontefract, please sit down. My name is Inspector Brown."

A cracked leather club chair sat across from the inspector and Percy sank into it wondering how she would ever get out. Her mug was angled perilously, and the blanket was pinched between her thumb and finger, fighting for freedom.

The inspector looked down at his notebook. "How did you come to be in the pantry at three o' clock in the morning?"

Percy repeated what she had just told Verity.

"Did you know the deceased?"

"That depends on what you mean by 'know'," began Percy. "I come to this house several times a year and as such have met Mrs. Barlow, but I don't send her Christmas cards."

The inspector's muddy eyes widened then morphed into another reluctant smile. "Indeed."

He dragged a pencil down the page. "So, you do *not* have a history with her?"

21

Percy's eyes snapped to attention. "Am I a suspect?"

His pale, dry lips twisted to one side. "I am not accusing you of anything just yet—"

"Just yet!" wailed Percy.

"Now, now Mrs. Pontefract. Let's not get upset." A deep crevice had formed between his eyes. "I am accusing no one, but the fact is that someone from this house hit the cook over the head with a rolling pin and you were the last one to see her."

"But she was already dead when I"—she gulped down bitter bile—"found her."

The inspector carefully placed his square chin in his palm. "It is a matter of procedure and from experience that we always take a closer look at the person that finds the body."

His tone was such that Percy half expected a cymbal crash or violin tremolo like on the radio dramas.

"If I *had* killed her, Inspector, why would I have laid on the floor right next to her?"

"Is that where you were when the alarm went up?" he asked.

"Yes! Check with Verity. After I, well"—she felt her cheeks get hot—"was sick, I screamed blue murder. I think I had a breakdown of sorts and my legs wouldn't work. I shrieked like an angry baby until they found me in the pantry."

"I shall take that into consideration," he said. "Now, can you think of anything else that might be useful? Did you hear or see anything that meant nothing at the time but since has concerned you?"

Her brain was still a vortex of nothingness, but she tried to put it in gear. She thought back to the noises she had heard on the landing. "I thought I heard a bird, which might have been a woman giggling, when I exited my room, and then I heard a couple of creaky floorboards, oh, and a door closing or something like it, when I was going into the water closet."

"Can you be more specific." His pencil was poised over the paper, his bleary eyes hopeful. "Did you see anyone?"

She huffed. "No. I waited to see if someone was there each time, but it was silent."

His shoulders sagged. "What about the kitchen? Anything unusual in there?"

"My eyes were so used to the dark by that point I didn't need to turn on the light. There is a half-curtain and the light from the moon—"

His fist thudded the desk. "I get it. Did you see anyone or anything?"

The inspector's roughness ruffled her feathers. "No. I saw and heard no one and everything was in its place." If he was going to be rude, she would temper her helpfulness.

"Not everything," said the inspector. "The rolling pin was in the pantry next to the body."

"Well, yes but I didn't need the rolling pin for a midnight snack. I would not have noticed."

"There were no other items, on the table, for example?" he asked.

Percy squeezed her eyes shut, remembering. "No. Nothing."

"I think that's all for now," he said, standing. "It goes without saying that you cannot go home until I give the all-clear. I may need to speak to you again."

Percy's stomach clenched. "Then I shall have to call my home. They are expecting me back. I have two young boys to think of."

"I'm sure you have some kind of maid or other who can take care of them, don't you?"

Percy was beginning to get annoyed by the inspector's narrow-minded attitude. "I have a cook who lives in, but I don't like to take advantage, Inspector." She placed the tea, which had gone cold, on the desk, let go her vice grip on the blanket, slammed a hand onto the arm of the chair and pushed down. Nothing. Pulling her feet in close to get better leverage, she tried again and this time raised her nether regions two inches from the leather seat. Grabbing the side of the desk she wrenched her body upright.

"Good day, Inspector." She spun and put her foot out, but it got tangled up in the tartan blanket and she stumbled forward, grasping for the door handle to steady herself. Risking a glance back, she observed the first genuine smile she had seen on the inspector's face and high-tailed it out of the office.

Chapter 5

She missed the warmth of the blanket and noticed she no longer had her tea. *I'm not going back in there after that exit!*

She shuffled across the foyer and up the stairs to her room. The bedclothes were scattered in a mess from hours before and she fought the longing to jump in, cover her head, and have a good cry.

Going to the wardrobe she found her clean underwear, sensible skirt, and wooly jumper. They all traditionally stayed over so they could stay up late and not worry about drinking.

Having changed out of her nightdress, she sat at the dressing table and reared back. Her skin was tear-stained and the miniscule amount of mascara she had worn was travelling down her cheeks by slow train. Why hadn't Verity told her? She opened her face cream and smoothed it on to wipe off the black streaks.

Her naturally frizzy hair now looked like a burr enlarged under a microscope. She tried pushing it down with her hands, but it was determined to disobey. She knew better than to brush it— that would make things a thousand times worse. Taking out a bushel of hairpins she set about trying to pin it up in some sort of organized fashion, but the finished product was not optimal as her hands were still shaking.

She needed company.

Entering the drawing room, Percy hesitated on the threshold, remembering the words of the inspector. *"Someone from this house hit the cook over the head with a rolling pin."* Running a suspicious eye over the group, she weighed her options. She considered running back to her room and locking the door but then she would be alone again. She decided that in her present state of shock, the benefit of being among friends outweighed the risk that one of them was the killer. Besides, if she stayed with the group, she would be safe. Murderers struck in private.

Verity was trying to get everyone to eat biscuits from a Christmas collection and Tom was pacing by the fireplace. Delicate Jemima looked as green as Percy felt and was being comforted by her husband, Bruce, while Ellen and Mark played cards. *Cards!* How could they do something so mundane at a time like this? Phoebe and Walter were both staring into their tea.

The inspector's words ringing in her head, Percy took one of the armchairs removed from the group, and examined her friends through a new lens, nibbling on a biscuit since she had not eaten since her mid-night snack.

She considered the lovely, if loud, Verity. She was confident and social and president of her children's parent-teacher association. Perhaps she had embezzled money from the orphan's fund and Mrs. Barlow had discovered it. She tried to cast Verity as desperate and able to wield a rolling pin at the head of the cook who had been her employee for the last five years. She just couldn't do it. Verity was like the mothers in housekeeping magazines, perfect hair, perfect figure, perfect life. No, it couldn't be her unless she had been possessed by an evil spirit.

She turned her gaze to Tom who was wearing a hole in the rug with his pacing. A handsome and athletic man in his youth, he had not aged particularly well. Percy suspected that being an accountant did that to a person—too much sitting. A hand-knitted jumper strained over his potbelly and his thinning hair showed more of his pale head beneath than the last time she had seen him. Accountants handled money too, didn't they? She had heard that money was one of the leading motives for murder. But Tom just wasn't the violent type. She remembered a summer garden party

26

where his son had fallen from a tree and broken his leg. Tom had come unglued. Verity had handled everything.

She mentally crossed the Howards off the list.

Bruce stood to get his wife another cup of tea. Unlike Tom, he had become more attractive with age. Tall, slim, athletic build. He glanced around the room at everyone, and Percy dropped her gaze, noticing a tea stain on her skirt. *Drat!* She licked her finger and tried to wipe it off, but it had dried into a stubborn stain.

By the time she looked up, Bruce's back was to her, returning to his seat. Both he and Piers were civil servants, but *he* didn't travel half so much. Civil servant. What did that even mean? It was an umbrella title for…she didn't really know what. Piers never talked specifics.

Bruce handed Jemima the cup and Percy noticed her hands were shaking as she took it. What did *she* have to be worried about? Percy was the one who had landed on the corpse. The inspector's words echoed in her head again. He had probably interviewed everyone by now and made the same solemn pronouncement about the murderer being one of them.

Jemima usually looked like a mousy librarian, all practical clothes and pearls, a neat bun rolled at the nape of her neck. But today she looked like she had been electrocuted, which helped Percy feel better about her own hair-raising appearance. Jemima had been a sweet and natural beauty when she married, but childbirth had left its mark on her figure as it had on Percy's.

Mark Richmond barked with laughter as he placed a card on the table pulling Percy's gaze from the Goodfellows. Ellen groaned and threw her hand down. They had hit the jackpot five years ago when an investment quadrupled in value. Mark had sunk the profit into an import business which took off and made them rich. What *did* he import? Percy could not remember. What if it was dodgy merchandise and Mrs. Barlow had found out? Mark suddenly locked eyes with her, and she conjured a false smile then hid her face in her cup for several minutes.

Needing another biscuit, she crossed the room, her eyes settling on Phoebe and Walter. They were her favorite of all the couples. Phoebe was kind and friendly and always made time to talk to Percy which could not really be said of the other three women. Even when Percy talked about her expanding stamp collection or the church roof fund, Phoebe was attentive. Walter was still very handsome and even though he had to give up tennis because of his artificial leg, he had managed to keep his youthful figure. *What kind of doctor was he?* A general practitioner? No. A surgeon. What if he had operated on Mrs. Barlow's relative and they had not survived and she confronted him?

Too many questions and not enough answers.

Percy's stomach growled again. Biscuits were not sufficient to curb her hunger. The clock said it was nine but no one had mentioned breakfast. Hoping that the body had been removed from the larder by now, she wandered out of the room and down the corridor to the closed kitchen. She knocked and when no one responded, cracked open the door.

"Hellooo! Can I come in?"

When no reply came, she opened the door wide. It was empty. She whisked the memory of the incident in the pantry away and went straight to the icebox. There sat the remains of the goose and the milk. She pushed the goose aside and grabbed the milk. Behind the meat was some pâté. *Perfect!*

Averting her gaze from the pantry, she retrieved the same loaf she had eaten during the night, found the knife and took everything to the table. As she pulled a chair out, it made a strange scraping sound. She crouched down. Moving her hand over the floor she found a small, red stone under one of the legs and slipped it into her pocket.

28

Dropping heavily into the chair, she cut a slice of bread and slathered on a generous helping of pâté. Closing her eyes in ecstasy, the smooth flavors flooded her mouth.

As she ate, her thoughts tiptoed to the cook. Did she have a family? Was she a mother? Would anyone miss her? She stuffed another mouthful in to smother the depressing thought.

She was confident that her *boys* would miss her. Would Piers? It was sometimes as if he forgot he had a wife.

Stop these maudlin thoughts.

One thing *was* sure. Verity would need to advertise for a new cook since Percy knew she was hopeless in the kitchen.

Having satisfied the hunger, fatigue walloped her. Percy had not gone back to bed since the horrifying discovery at three o'clock. She slogged her way up the stairs, rounded the corridor, and stopped short. An intense conversation was under way.

"Don't be so bally insensitive!" hissed Verity Howard. "The poor woman is hardly cold."

The other person was much more discreet. Percy could not make out who it was, though the deep register led her to believe it was a man. Tom?

"We have to give her a proper funeral. She never married, and I think she was an only child. It's the least we can do."

Percy strained her ears. All she could make out was a deep, urgent mumbling but if they were discussing a funeral it had to be Tom. Perhaps he was suggesting advertising for a new cook and Verity thought it too early.

The voices moved farther away, and Percy risked a quick look round the wall. She was too late. Feeling suddenly vulnerable, she dashed along the hall to her room and slid in as if she were being stalked. Trembling fingers locked the door. Her pulse was pounding in her ears, and she didn't wait for it to get back to normal before jumping into the unmade bed and pulling the covers over her head. The curtains were still pulled, the room dark, her stomach full. Within seconds she was out.

Crash!

Percy jolted awake in terror.

Chapter 6

Percy lay stock still, her heart beating erratically with alarm.

She strained her ears. Nothing. She must have dreamed it.

The room was dark, but light peeped around the edges of the drapes revealing dark shadows. Mouth dry, she reached for the glass tumbler on the bedside table, but her fingers fluttered in air. She lifted her head. No glass. Rolling her large frame to the edge of the bed, she spotted the cup on its side, spewing water onto the rug.

One mystery solved. I must have knocked it off in my sleep.

She rolled back. The clock had phosphorescence and Percy could see that the time was two in the afternoon. *Two!* She needed to call the boys.

Rushing out of bed, she flew down the stairs to the telephone. Rather than being housed in a dedicated cabinet, the modern looking instrument was sitting on a dainty table in the hall, a chair beside it.

"Surrey, 721," she gasped into the receiver. Perhaps she *should* take up tennis or something if she was this out of shape.

"Pontefract residence," said the voice of Mrs. Appleby. All at once Percy felt emotional. She swallowed down a big lump.

"Mrs. Appleby, it's just me. How are the boys?"

"Well, young master William got into my golden syrup without permission, so he's up in his room and master Bartholomew is reading."

"Oh, I'm sorry about Will," she said. "He's got my sweet tooth." She picked at a bit of pâté that was clinging to her jumper, having survived her nap. "Look, there's been a bit of a doodah here, and I need to stay a bit longer. Is that going to be a problem?"

"Is everything alright?" Mrs. Appleby had a sixth sense. "Of course, the boys are fine with me."

"Verity just needs me to help with some things. I simply wanted to let you know not to expect me home today. With a bit of luck, I should be back tomorrow."

"Thank you for letting me know, Mrs. Pontefract. Would you like to speak to the boys?"

Percy did not trust herself to keep it together. "I'm sure they're busy. Just tell them I've been delayed. Goodbye." She ended the call abruptly, feeling her eyes sting.

Sitting, staring at the paneled wall, she gathered her composure and walked back to the drawing room. Everyone was there, talking. No, not everyone. Tom Howard was absent.

A tea set sat on a little coffee table and Percy went to get herself a cup. She winced. It was far too strong. She ladled in more cream and sugar.

Jemima scooted over to make room for Percy and lifted her finger to point to Percy's eye. "You have some...uh..."

Percy took a napkin and wiped her eye leaving a black streak on the fabric. She wondered if mascara was really worth the effort. "Thanks."

"Have you been asleep?" asked Jemima.

"Yes. Why do you ask?"

"Your, um, hair. It's a bit smooshed on the side."

Percy realized she hadn't even looked in the mirror when she awoke. She tried to run fingers through her hair, but they got snagged on all the pins. She patted her do instead. She must look an absolute fright. "Thanks."

"I don't know how you could sleep, though," said Jemima, wiping at a non-existent tear. "It is simply awful! Awful!"

"I hadn't slept since three this morning. I was exhausted," retorted Percy.

32

"Me neither," said Jemima in her patient voice. "But I know I cannot sleep with a dead woman in the house."

"The body is still here?" asked Percy, thinking back to her snack in the kitchen, her tone a couple of octaves higher than usual. She shivered.

"Why do we call a dead person a *body*? It is so undignified," said Jemima, brushing crumbs from her gray skirt. "Yes, *she's* still in the pantry since it's cold. Unhygienic, I say.

Percy's stomach began to revolt. She pressed a hand to it and swallowed hard. "Why haven't the police taken it—her away?"

"Something about needing a van. It's already in use," Jemima explained.

"Did you know her?" asked Percy.

"Who? Mrs. Barlow? No. She was just the cook. I only came here once a year for the Christmas party. You?"

"Same. We come a couple more times a year—"

"You do? I wonder why *we're* not invited?" demanded Jemima, seeming to forget about the corpse.

Sticky.

"It's just a couple of garden parties. Nothing special." This was not entirely true, but Percy had already put her enormous foot in her mouth. "I don't really *know* Mrs. Barlow. Isn't it a shame that staff are treated as second class citizens. Why don't we talk to them?" Percy did not treat Mrs. Appleby like that. She was considered part of the family. A surrogate mother at times.

"I was wondering the same thing," murmured Jemima. "When I get home, I'm going to sit down and have a cup of tea with my housekeeper, cook and the maids."

The truth was that Percy relied on Mrs. Appleby for company and friendship. With both boys gone and Piers away for work she was lonely and often ate dinner in the kitchen with her sympathetic cook.

"Are you nervous to stay here?" asked Percy.

A shot of alarm diffused over Jemima's bland face and she whispered, "You mean because someone here killed the poor woman?"

"Exactly. You have your husband, but I'm here alone."

"Yes, where is dear Piers?"

"I wish I knew," huffed Percy. "*Away* is all he said."

Jemima sent daggers to the other occupants of the room. "One of *them*—a murderer!"

It was an unsettling feeling, but Percy was still more disturbed. She knew it had not been her, but she could not be certain that it had not been Jemima.

"The police will figure it out," Percy assured her. "I need another cup. You?" This was a lie but Jemima's nervy manner and suspicions were making Percy anxious.

"No thanks."

Percy got up and having poured herself another potent cup, decided to sit by someone else. Phoebe and Verity were chatting on the couch.

"—so very sad there is no family," said Verity.

"Did Mrs. Barlow not have anyone?" asked Percy.

"No. She just used the title 'Mrs.' as is custom for older female servants. She once told me she was engaged in the late 1880s, but her fiancé died of consumption. Fancy devoting yourself to someone's memory to the point that you sacrifice your future happiness?" said Verity.

"Romantic nonsense," said Phoebe. "Who would sacrifice having children and a husband for the memory of a dead love? Sounds like a bad novel. I bet there was more to it than that."

Phoebe made a sensible point. But could it have any bearing on her murder? Percy didn't see how.

Verity puckered her lips with disapproval. "She's dead, Phoebe. Show some respect."

"Well, excuse me," said Phoebe tartly. "I'm just giving my opinion."

Percy felt like a cat at a dog show. "If she has no family, who will take care of the funeral arrangement?" She was hoping to deflect the touchy conversation in another direction.

"We will. She served us well for five years. It's the least we can do," said Verity.

"That's very generous of you," said Percy.

"Anyone would do the same," Verity replied, modestly.

She looked to see if Phoebe looked penitent when Percy noticed she was absent a pearl earring. "Uh, you're missing—" She reached to her own ear lobe and Phoebe's fingers followed suit.

"Cripes! They're my grandmother's. I rarely take them out. They're worth a fortune," shrieked Phoebe.

"I can get everyone to search, if you like," offered Verity.

"Would you? I'll check my room." Phoebe jumped up and ran out the door.

Percy was about to say that she had found a red crystal when Verity clapped her hands. "Everyone! Phoebe is missing a pearl earring. I propose we all search this room, the dining room, stairs, and hallways."

Soon everyone was bottoms up, examining every inch of the drawing room. When they came up empty, Verity divided people into areas. Percy had the upstairs landing.

She mounted the stairs where Walter was already searching with his hands and dropped to her knees.

"I had them re-valued recently for the insurance company," he said. "They're worth a bomb!"

"So, I heard," responded Percy, scouring the carpet runner. Within two minutes she had found a shilling, a hair pin, a piece of a note that had been torn with the partial words 'et me. 2' written on it, and a dressmaking pin. No earring.

As she and Walter were about to make their way down to report, Phoebe appeared at the bottom of the stairs, tension branded on her features. *Wasn't she supposed to be searching her room?*

"No luck here," he said.

"Nothing in the k—hall either," said Phoebe.

"I found a red crystal in the kitchen earlier," Percy offered.

Phoebe's face went blank. "But I'm looking for a pearl."

Chapter 7

The missing earring did not turn up and the usually upbeat Phoebe sulked all through a sparse lunch. Her husband had pointed out that the earrings were insured but she uncharacteristically snapped back that insurance could not replace the intrinsic value of the pearls.

She was not the only one who was disagreeable. Prohibited from returning home, everyone seemed to be on edge. It was becoming apparent that you *could* have too much of a good thing.

Percy was no exception. She needed some space from her prickly friends and excused herself to use the lavatory. The upstairs bathroom faced the sloping back garden, and Percy peered out to see how short they had clipped their roses. She had been bothered for some time by the idea that she had cut hers too low and that they would struggle to bloom in the summer. As she peeped out, a movement by the shed caught her eye. The bird's eye view gave her clear sight of a man she did not recognize. He was standing with his back to the shed as if he were waiting for someone but didn't want to be seen from the house. Having little else to do and knowing she could not be seen, Percy stared unabashed. The man was smoking a cigarette and rocking on his feet. Every so often, he would sneak a peek around the shed then pull quickly back. He glanced at his watch constantly.

The handle on the bathroom door jiggled sending Percy jumping out of her skin. She put a hand to her chest. "Just a minute," she said, flushing the toilet again and keeping her eye trained on the shed.

Just as she felt she could no longer occupy the lavatory without raising eyebrows, a flash of purple scarf sped across the garden and threw itself at the man. A quick, passionate embrace followed and then the woman turned and ran back to the house. As she ran it began to rain and the woman looked up.

It was Verity!

Percy pulled violently back from the window, her heart hammering.

The perfect Verity was having an affair?

Percy was the world's worst at pretense. How would she ever be able to act naturally after witnessing her friend's infidelity?

She stretched her neck high and stalked out of the bathroom. It was Tom waiting and Percy felt the skin on her cheeks burn. He examined her face.

"Everything alright, Percy?"

"Oh yes!" she said, putting a hand to the hot skin. "Just feeling a little warm." She pulled at her thick sweater.

"Jolly good," he said, passing her and closing the door.

Phew!

She cringed. Every part of her was now itching to leave, but until the police gave everyone the 'all clear' that was not about to happen. She wondered if she would be interviewed again. What if she wasn't? As she plodded down the stairs, holding tightly to the banister, she considered whether the clandestine relationship had any bearing on the murder and if she should mention it to the police. Or was that disloyal to an old friend? But there had been a murder and in Verity's house.

She wandered to Tom's study where the surly inspector had set up shop and knocked.

"Come in!"

She poked her head through the door.

"Yes?" He growled, sounding like a bear who had just woken up from hibernation. She felt her spirits shrink. Perhaps this was a bad idea.

"I may have some pertinent information," she croaked, clutching her throat in an attempt to make her voice work properly.

"Let's hear it then." Could he be more grumpy?

Percy slunk over to the infamous chair she had occupied before and told the inspector what she had just witnessed.

The inspector's wiry eyebrows danced over his eyes. "Really? I mean, are you sure?"

"Positive. She looked up and I got a full view of her face."

"Did you recognize the man?" he asked.

"Never seen him before," she replied truthfully.

"You understand that I shall have to question Mrs. Howard about it?"

Percy's stomach dropped off a cliff. "Does she have to know it was me that saw her?"

"No. I'll just keep it vague," said the inspector.

"Th...thank you." She struggled out of the chair, and lurched for the door. Once out, she leaned her back against the wood, trying to rein in her racing heart.

Walter ambled by holding a whiskey and looking like he had the weight of the world on his shoulders. He nodded in her direction. Would he guess her treachery? She quickly slipped back to the sitting room scanning for Verity. She was absent, and Percy felt a jolt of relief. A large jigsaw puzzle had been laid out on the coffee table and Percy gravitated to it like a drowning man lunges for a life ring. Jemima and Phoebe were already hard at work.

"You alright, Percy?" asked Phoebe.

Why was everyone asking her if she was alright?

"You look a bit peaky," Phoebe continued.

"Just antsy to get home. The boys have been gone all term and I had plans." Ha! She was better at lying than she thought. That actually sounded credible. *And even after I stumbled into a corpse!*

"I know what you mean," said Jemima. "I was supposed to take the children to Oxford Street to see the Christmas display windows. It's something of a tradition."

Percy picked up a piece of sky, held it for a second, and placed it back on the table. The picture was a Mediterranean Greek seascape.

"Where is our hostess?" said Percy, still worried about how she would react when she first saw her. The two women exchanged a glance and Phoebe said, "I believe she's on the phone with the mortuary."

Percy's heart rate slowed. "Oh, yes. I'm sure there's a lot to arrange. Silly me." She picked up another piece of the puzzle that seemed to be surf but since the whole picture was of cloudless, blue sky and azure ocean, she replaced it. *Who had chosen such an uninteresting puzzle?*

She let her eyes wander around the room since Verity was absent. Bruce was dressed dashingly in a crisp, white shirt and highly pressed slacks, his full hair brushed back. He looked at least eight years younger than his homely wife. He was at ease, reading a book and ignoring everyone around him.

Walter Valentine entered, still holding the whiskey tumbler that was now empty, deep in thought. Frown lines rippled across his attractive face. His stooped posture betrayed his stress and as she watched she noticed that his smooth hands were trembling. Nerves? That could not be a good condition for a surgeon.

He and Phoebe had been the envy of everyone in their youth, but today, he looked like what he was. A middle-aged doctor with a mortgage. She glanced back at the lovely Phoebe who was looking steadfastly at the puzzle on the table.

Ellen and Mark were both seated on a couch but faced away from each other as though they'd had a falling out. Mark was nursing his own tumbler of whiskey while Ellen ignored him, dressed in a Chanel number that made it seem like she was trying to look younger than she was.

Tom was missing too. Perhaps he was helping his wife with the funeral arrangements or perhaps...

40

She experienced a sudden gut punch of homesickness. Not for the bricks and mortar but for her boys. "If you would excuse me," she said standing and knocking over the chair. "I'm going to call home."

Closing the door on the somber group in the sitting room, she crossed the hallway to get to the front entry that held the telephone praying that she did not bump into Verity. As she passed a small library, she caught sight of Tom, head in his hands. Guilt punched her again.

When Mrs. Appleby picked up the phone, she asked if she could speak to William. He was always a good pick me up.

"Hello, Mummy. We're playing forts in the dining room."

She felt a rush of motherly affection and swallowed it down before it fell over onto her cheeks. "How lovely! Did you sleep well, darling?"

"Bartie read me some adventure stories so I had a bit of trouble falling asleep, but the stories were *so* good! I had dreams of being a pirate on a ship. When are you coming home?"

Her heart constricted. "I'm not sure, sweetheart. Hopefully tomorrow, which isn't too far away, is it?"

"No, but why can't you come home now?" he pleaded. "There's new snow and you promised we could go tobogganing."

"Because Mrs. Howard needs my help with something. That is the only thing that could keep me away. I'll come home as soon as I can. Be good for Mrs. Appleby. Is Bartie there?"

"Hold on!"

She heard the clatter of the receiver on the telephone table and steeled herself for an awkward conversation with her oldest son.

"Yes." There was so much emotion packed into that one little word. Accusation, embarrassment, hostility.

"Hello darling, just checking in. How're things going?" She squinted her eyes as she waited for his answer.

"Fine." So, it was to be monosyllables today.

"I was just telling William I shall be delayed a little longer, but I know I can count on you to hold down the fort." She hated the hint of desperation in her tone.

"Hmmm."

"Thank you for reading to William last night. It helps him sleep." She grasped at the straw Will had thrown her.

"Look, I have to go. William is trying to force entry into my citadel."

A ripple of disappointment trickled down her chest. "Oh! Alright, then. Goodbye sw—Bartie."

The beeps across the line sounded in her ear as she sat holding the receiver to her head for a few seconds before hanging the smooth piece onto its hook. She bit her lip. The trauma of the morning hit her with full force and she felt a fierce need to talk to Piers. But as usual, she did not know where he was.

Wiping her cheek, she lumbered down the hall back to the thorny drawing room passing Tom, who was still hunched over in his chair in an attitude of despair.

Chapter 8

Percy's mind was a jumble of new paradigms. She had always thought Tom and Verity had a good marriage, but the man in the garden had not been a figment of her imagination. Did Tom know? Was that the actual cause of his douleur?

Percy halted as she came face to face with a jolly Verity telling everyone that tea was ready and not to expect too much because it was the inexperienced kitchen maid who had prepared the meal and she was a nervous wreck. Percy averted her conscience-stricken eyes as they filed into the dining room that still bore the vestiges of the celebration from the night before. How could things have changed so drastically in so short a time? Verity scraped up the remains of the crackers and dumped them beside the sideboard and Percy realized that she hadn't seen any other servants. There had been no maids to clean up after their celebration the night before.

The 'meal' was cold cuts, cheese, and bread and was most welcome as Percy's stomach grumbled. She delicately placed slice after slice on her plate, her mouth watering in anticipation of the farmhouse cheddar, whose pungent fragrance hit her senses before the food. A spoonful of green olives completed the simple meal but as Percy turned, one of the little green balls rolled right off her plate. Knees cracking, she squatted down to retrieve it at the very same time Ellen was getting something from her handbag. A million sparkles caught Percy's eye, and her gaze landed on the most ravishing diamond bracelet she had ever beheld.

Ellen locked eyes with Percy, shook her head and thrust the bracelet back in her bag. *What was that about?* Percy put a finger to her lips before standing up to find a seat at the table.

Did everyone here have a bally secret?

Now afraid to make eye contact with Verity, *or* Ellen, Percy concentrated all her attention on her meal. Tom had not appeared, which did not surprise Percy. He was in a better mood for strong spirits.

"Where did you say Piers was?" asked Mark, casually.

"I didn't," she replied talking to her knife. "He travels so much and is pretty vague."

"Huh," responded Mark. His grunt hit every note on the scale from do to do. What did he mean?

She had always accepted her husband's responses at face value, but the last twenty-four hours had upended her faith in the goodness of human nature and now doubts niggled at her. What if he was vague because *he* was having an affair? She thought of her tall, reedy, balding spouse with the tiny round spectacles and laughed inside. *Not* the affair type. He was a blubbering mess around women. He had hardly been able to ask her out all those years ago. In fact, *she* had really been the one to ask him. It had taken him a further four months to even hold her hand. She had been on the verge of breaking up with him, thinking he didn't like her all that much, but before she could follow through, he had taken her hand at the opera and everything had changed. It was clammy and cold, but she hadn't cared. It had taken another three months to kiss her and they had bumped noses on their first attempt, knocking off his glasses. No, whatever Piers was doing, he was definitely *not* having an affair. It must be this tense atmosphere making her suspicious.

Eyes now trained squarely on her fork, she asked Mark, "What is it you are importing these days?"

"This and that," he said avoiding the question entirely. "It's an ever-changing game."

Risking a glance up, she connected with Ellen, whose face was engraved with fear. Percy tried to convey that she would keep Ellen's confidence, but the weird interaction reminded her that the couple had been ignoring each other with open hostility for most of the morning. She ducked her head back to her plate and hoped the excruciating meal would soon be over.

Unable to face the idea of more barbed conversations in the drawing room, Percy made her way to the kitchen to see if she could at least offer some condolences to the young maid who now had the responsibility of feeding them all. On her way, she passed Phoebe scribbling a note in the hall. Being so tall she could not help seeing the words, 'meet me' before Phoebe put a hand over the writing.

Phoebe's face squeezed into a phony smile. "I remembered I have to settle a bill for the butcher so I'm sending him a message since I am not home to take care of it." The fabricated smile did not reach her eyes and Percy hurried on, dismayed at having to juggle more dishonesty in her brain.

In the cold kitchen, the wiry maid was staring at a cup of tea, her eyes and nose red, a scrunched handkerchief by her cup. She looked up with empty eyes like those of an opium addict.

"I just wanted to let you know that you did a great job with tea. Splendid!" gushed Percy, embarrassed by the girl's mourning. "What's on the menu for dinner?" *Drat!* She shouldn't have put pressure on the poor girl.

The smooth skin on the young maid's face crumpled like burning paper. "We don't 'ave enough food for everyone. You's was all s'posed to leave today."

Percy slid onto a chair across the table from the girl and patted her hand. "There, there. Perhaps I can help?"

Wet lashes lifted with hope. "Could you?"

"Of course! I help my own cook all the time. Sit tight while I have a look in the larder."

Seized by a sudden panic at returning to the place of her recent ordeal, Percy hesitated.

"The, uh, body. Has it been removed?"

45

The maid sniffed. "Yes. They came to get her an hour ago."

Memories of the nightmare rose like phantoms and Percy had to grab the back of the chair. *Get a grip!* She forced her feet forward and pulled on the door of the larder, heart hammering. She took a quick look around the shelves and found plenty of canned meats and winter vegetables in baskets. To her surprise, a couple of pheasants were hanging in the back corner and Percy grabbed them off the hook and hurried out of the ghostly room.

"These will do," she said, and offered one to the girl. "You can make a roast or use the meat for a hearty soup."

Half smile, half tears, the girl accepted the bird.

"What's your name?" asked Percy, pulling a newspaper out of the bin to put the discarded feathers on, grabbing a handful of down and pulling hard.

"Martha, m'am."

"Martha. And how long have you worked for the Howards?"

As they both got into a rhythm of plucking, the girl seemed to calm down. "About a year. Started when I was fourteen, just out of school."

"And do you like it here?"

A slight hesitation. "Oh, yes. I know when I have a good place. My friends don't have it 'alf so good. Mrs. Barlow was so kind. Like a mother to me, really, since my own mum passed away." Her voice broke. "I can't believe she's gone…"

"Are there no other servants?"

"Not anymore. They let the housemaids go a few months back and the gardener. We just have a man who comes once a week to keep the garden in shape."

Interesting.

Percy slipped another sheet of newspaper out and spread it on the table to collect the peelings from the vegetables.

46

As she took up a knife and dropped the first peel, her eyes caught on a small headline.

Doctor Under Investigation For Accidental Death.

As Martha chatted, Percy surreptitiously read the small article. An un-named doctor had performed a surgery that left an otherwise young, healthy patient dead. After a thorough inquiry, it was determined that the doctor had arrived for the surgery drunk. Charges were pending.

"Don't you think so?" asked Martha.

Percy nodded, hoping it was the correct reaction.

They continued talking while they worked and by the end of the conversation there were two dressed pheasants, peeled potatoes, carrots, and parsnips.

"It has been nice making your acquaintance, Martha. I'd best get back."

"Thank you, m'am. I'm feeling much more confident now."

But Percy could not say the same. Something about the article she had read had got its hooks into her mind and would not let go.

Chapter 9

Still unable to face going back to the drawing room, Percy decided to take a turn around the Howard's large garden. Pulling on her thick, red wooly hat over her smashed locks, she shrugged into the old, fur-lined leather coat and stuffed her hands into thick gloves. When she stepped outside, the frigid air bit at her face. The dormant lawn was covered with a thin layer of frost that had not melted, the blades of grass poking through like green fingers.

She crunched along a paved path to a round pond whose fountain had been turned off. A layer of thin ice blurred the image of the large, red koi floating beneath the surface. She stood fascinated, watching them swim as if through an unearthly veil.

Hearing a crack, she looked around her. Could it be the welcomed intruder? Seeing no one, she wandered over to the potting shed where several sets of footprints were clearly visible. One set small and dainty, the other left by hefty work boots. Here was proof she had not imagined the illicit rendezvous. Turning to leave, her eye caught on the glass of one of the dirty windows. A finger-drawn, lop-sided heart bearing the initials 'V' and 'B' was clear in the grime.

Sloppy.

She continued on to the graveyard of vegetables, now stretching out withered leaves like mermaid hair along the ground, and on to the copse of trees that divided the Howard property from the neighbor behind. The same boot prints were clearly visible coming out from and going back through the trees. She about-faced and followed the trail of prints which kept to the sides of the garden, hugging the fence and leading to the shed.

What further proof did she need? *Poor Tom.* No wonder he looked like the weight of the world was on his shoulders.

The unmistakable crunch of footsteps on frozen grass drew near and Percy braced. With her size, there was absolutely no chance of hiding.

"Percy!" gasped Verity. "I thought I saw someone out here." She cast a sheepish glance at the heart on the glass. "What are you doing?"

"I've been cooped up for too long. I needed some fresh air." Her eyes darted everywhere, uncontrollably. "I should be sledding with the boys about now. It's one of our traditions. Sledding and hot cocoa by the fire while I read a Christmas story." She was babbling but couldn't stop herself. "Do you have traditions with the children?"

Verity's eyes bore thin lines of anxiety and her strained jaw betrayed her worry. "Um, I'm not sure if you saw something…"

Percy's eyes bulged. Was now the time for candor? She decided it was not and remained silent.

Verity grabbed the bare skin at her neck and sighed, her breath forming a cloud of steam. "You did." She cleared her throat and kicked the ground. "It's just a silly fling. A bit of excitement, you know. Nothing serious. Tom…hasn't been himself lately."

Percy dropped her gaze, reflected shame crawling across her skin. "Certainly none of my business," she muttered, though she was actually mortified by her friend's treachery.

"Well, I'm hoping I can count on your discretion, dear. I'm about to break it off, as a matter of fact. No need to bother Tom with the details, eh?"

Percy examined the moist, white toes of her boots. "Of course."

"Glad that's settled then." Verity spun on her heels and plodded back to the house leaving Percy reeling.

49

The inspector had asked them all to provide their fingerprints. He had stopped short of accusing one of the house party, but it was implied and had cast an even deeper pall over the group of friends.

When Percy re-entered the study, forgetting to knock, she glimpsed a map of the house on the detective's desk with initials and times by certain rooms. According to the map, no one had been out of their room at three in the morning but the cook and Percy, which she knew must be a lie because she had heard the creak of footsteps right before entering the bathroom. And the giggle.

Inspector Brown jerked and seeing her staring, slipped a book over the map.

"Fingers please."

He took her over-sized hand and rolled her thumb on a pad of black ink. "Someone is lying," she said, being brave. "I definitely heard someone in the hall when I went to the loo."

He leveled his gaze at her. "Everyone is lying, Mrs. Pontefract. It is a fact of the job."

"Well, *I'm* not!" she declared as he rolled her thumb across a card.

His eyes narrowed. "Are you not even bending the truth a little?"

She placed a hand on her heart. "No!" She followed the detective's gaze to see that she had used the blackened hand and now had a smudge of black ink on her favorite sweater. "Bother!"

The inspector handed her a damp rag, but it only made things worse.

"I wager you have noticed things among your friends that you have not disclosed to me," Inspector Brown pushed.

"I told you about Verity and the stranger in the garden. She has verified it, actually. I was having a wander about and found some very masculine boot prints by the shed and a juvenile heart drawn into the dust on the window."

"Yes, thank you. I've already added him to the list of suspects." If one could sound ungrateful while thanking someone, he did.

Percy's heart stopped. "I promised I wouldn't tell Tom."

"And you haven't." The inspector smiled, his bristly mustache wrinkling on his lip.

"Can you be discreet about it?" she pleaded. "Can you not question her about it in private, instead of broaching the topic with Tom? I don't think he knows and it might break him. She said she's going to break it off, anyway."

"Ah, huh. That's what they all say." The inspector all but rolled his eyes.

"Yes, I suppose they do," agreed Percy with flailing spirits.

The inspector took her index finger while staring deep into her soul.

"Oh, alright!" she blustered, caving under the pressure. "Tom looks like he's on the verge of a mental collapse, Ellen has a very valuable diamond bracelet in her purse that she wants to keep from her husband, Mark can never give a straight answer about what it is he imports, and Phoebe was penning a note that she says is for the butcher but looked more like an invitation to a secret assignation—"

"A what?" asked the inspector.

Percy sniffed. "You know, an illicit meeting. Oh, and Walter is drinking heavily." She threw her head back. "There! That's all I know."

The inspector leaned back with a satisfied smile. "See, that wasn't so bad."

"Then why do I feel like a rotten backstabber?"

"You haven't accused anyone of anything. You have merely given valuable background to one of his majesty's law officers. It is called doing your duty, Mrs. Pontefract."

A craving to bite her nails hit, but every finger now had ink on it. She curled her hands into fists.

"When can we go home?" she asked.

"I've interviewed everyone and once I've taken all the fingerprints, I don't see the need to keep you all here any longer. I know where everybody lives." His left eye was twitching, and she jumped up and fled the room with a huge, ugly knot in her chest.

Panting, she ran up to her room and packed so that the minute he gave them permission to leave, she would be ready.

She was finding it hard to breathe.

Chapter 10

"Mummy!" shrieked William, crashing into her legs and causing her to stumble. The heat of his little body transferring to hers, warmed her chilled heart. When did the innocent acceptance of childhood morph into the umbridge of pre-adolescence? It had shocked her out of complacency with Bartie, and she did not want to be blindsided again. She would cherish every sticky moment.

She ruffled William's light hair. "It's so good to be home."

The scent of steak and kidney pudding wafted from the kitchen and her stomach jumped in delight as she shuffled to the coat rack, William still clinging to her as if she were a life buoy.

"Did you have fun?" he asked, as Percy noticed with sadness his summer freckles were almost gone.

A creak from above sent her glance up and she caught a brief glimpse of plaid on the landing.

"Fun? I suppose so." She hung her hat and scarf, wriggling out of her coat, the delectable barnacle still stuck fast.

"If I was invited to a Christmas party, I would be sure to have oodles of fun...and pudding."

"Well, I *did* do that. And goose. The food was delicious." She rubbed her tummy for emphasis causing a cascade of giggles to spill from his adorable little mouth.

Sliding down, she pulled him into a bear hug, drinking in the boyish perfume of his hair.

"That you Mrs. P?" A shrill voice like a truck with bad breaks echoed down the hall.

"We'd better go, Wills," she said, unwilling to peel the little boy from her person and waiting until he broke the hold.

"Coming!" she cried back.

The kitchen of the rambling farmhouse was her favorite part of the house. A sturdy black Aga sat like an austere monk in the corner, filling the large room with heat. An ancient beam above held shiny, brass horse bits. Winter sun shone through the casement window that overlooked the ghost of a garden, casting a pool of light on the huge, battered oak table that anchored the room, an heirloom from her paternal grandmother. Happy childhood memories at her Granny Crabtree's flooded her mind every time she saw it. A large, cast-iron potholder sat over the table, displaying copper pans shining like soldiers in armor ready for culinary battle. A fire on the opposite wall from the Aga crackled and popped merrily, filling the air with the comforting smell of firewood and sending the odd spark flying onto the hearth.

"I thought I heard you," said Mrs. Appleby. "Your stomach must have known the pie is almost done. Have a nice time, did you?"

The old cook pulled on thick oven mitts and using a special cast iron hook, opened the bottom door of the Aga, withdrawing a heavy dish topped with a golden, shiny crust. Rich brown gravy bubbled at the edges.

Percy's eyes closed in ecstasy. "Mmm! You are a wonder, Mrs. Appleby."

"Master Bartholomew!" the cook shrieked. Percy held onto her hands to prevent them covering her ears. Mrs. Appleby was the only person allowed to call her older son by his full name. "Lunch is ready!"

Percy and William dropped into the oak spindle chairs surrounding the table which had been set with merry, red gingham place mats and green serviettes held by holly rings. The pie continued to steam and bubble as Mrs. Appleby brought candied roast carrots and parsnips to the table and handed out hot potatoes in their jackets, crisped by the magic of the Aga.

54

As the cook cut into the flaky pastry top of the pie, Bartie slid in.

"Hello, darling," said Percy, to which Bartie grunted a reply. It was more than she had hoped for.

"Here you go, Mrs. P.," said Mrs. Appleby, deftly extracting a generous slice and shifting it onto Percy's plate.

Percy inhaled for a full ten seconds. "You are worth your weight in gold, Mrs. Appleby." She ladled the roasted vegetables onto her plate and slit open the crusty potato, drowning it with fresh butter. "Bon appetit!"

William and Mrs. Appleby chatted about what they had been doing while Percy was away as a glowering Bartie ate in silence. She wished she knew how to penetrate his spiky shell.

The tender meat dissolved in Percy's mouth as she listened to the happy chatter.

"Raspberry cobbler?" asked the cook when they were all done. "Canned in September from the bushes in the garden."

Percy patted her stomach. "I'm too full at present but I'm putting in an order for an hour from now."

"Me too!" agreed William, groaning.

"How about you, Master Bartholomew?" asked the cook.

With a face like an angry dog, he barked, "I'll have some later." He tipped his scowl to his mother. "May I leave the table?"

"Haven't you forgotten something?" she asked.

Bartie frowned then his brow cleared. "Thank you for the delicious food, Mrs. Appleby."

"My pleasure, young man."

He plodded out of the room and thundered up the stairs.

Percy shrugged at Mrs. Appleby who shrugged back.

"Thank you for the dinner. May I go and play with my tin soldiers?" asked William in a voice as sweet as Bartie's was sour.

"Of course."

William slithered off his chair as Percy kissed his cheek, and out into the comfy lounge.

"Now, tell me what happened," demanded Mrs. Appleby, putting a kettle on to boil.

"Is it that obvious?" asked Percy, pushing her chair back and stretching her long legs.

"Well, first you can't come home, and then you arrive looking like a bear with a toothache."

Percy clasped her hands in front of her lips. "Someone murdered the cook."

Mrs. Appleby dropped the lid of the kettle into the sink. "Murdered!"

Percy put a finger to her lips, eyes anxious.

"My apologies," whispered Mrs. Appleby. "But of all the things I had imagined it to be, *that* was not one of them." She put the kettle on the Aga and sat next to Percy, clasping her rough hands together. "Tell me all about it."

While the kettle boiled, the tealeaves steeped, and the tea was poured through the strainer, Percy unloaded.

"Well, I never! What a lot of bad behavior," tutted Mrs. Appleby, her wrinkled face tight with disapproval. "They should all know better!"

"Indeed! But what about the poor cook?" remarked Percy.

Mrs. Appleby shook her head. "And what a way to die! With your own rolling pin!"

"And poor me for stumbling over her," Percy added, craving a little sympathy.

Mrs. Appleby patted her arm. "My giddy aunt! Terrible! Terrible!"

"It was worse because I was alone. I couldn't even go to Piers for a comforting hug," she explained. Though, she wondered if he would have been able to produce one had he been there.

"No wonder you looked like death warmed up—" Mrs. Appleby wrinkled her nose as her lips turned down. "Sorry, not the best adage given the circumstances."

But something about it tickled Percy's funny bone and she began to chuckle, then guffaw, then shriek with laughter.

Am I hysterical? She half expected Mrs. Appleby to slap her across the face.

William popped his head around the door. "What's so funny?"

Mrs. Appleby flicked a tea towel at him. "Nothing you would find amusing." He disappeared again.

"Excuse me!" Percy begged when she was done. "But I think I needed to get that out."

"No apology necessary," said Mrs. Appleby, pushing a pin back into her white bun. "Who do *you* think did it?"

"Me? I haven't spent a lot of time thinking about it," admitted Percy. "It was hard enough to remain calm with the notion that *one* of them had probably done it."

"Oh, come on! Cooped up with all those people after a murder and you didn't consider each one of them?"

Percy rested her chin in her palm. "Well, maybe a bit."

"Out with it," encouraged the cook.

"Well, the hosts, Verity and Tom, obviously know their way around the kitchen best but what possible motive would they have? It seems rather a severe way of dealing with theft or the like. And besides, they offered to cover the cost of the funeral. That would be unlikely if they had killed her for cause, don't you think?"

"Happy to say I couldn't tell you the mind of a murderer." Mrs. Appleby chuckled as she pushed a wisp of hair out of her face. "What about Verity's fancy man? Could he have come into the kitchen for a scandalous tryst and the cook interrupted them?"

Percy considered this scenario. The pair had certainly been sneaking around outside but she couldn't envision the larder as a romantic assignation spot. "It's possible but unlikely in my opinion."

"Alright then, who's next?" asked the cook, taking a sip of her tea.

"Jemima and Bruce Goodfellow. Jemima is always nervy, but I'm not sure she was more so after the murder. She has no backbone and committing a murder, especially one in the heat of the moment, would have undone her." She considered the handsome, dapper Bruce with his diamond cufflinks. "Bruce would have the nerve I think, but what would be his motive?"

"Let's shelve them for the moment, then," suggested Mrs. Appleby, her expression betraying that she was thoroughly enjoying all the gossip.

"Then there's Ellen and Mark Richmond. Something is definitely wrong there. They're usually the life and soul of the party, but they were pretty subdued after the murder. Animosity toward each other was rippling off them. No, not right after the murder." She remembered them playing cards as if nothing had happened. "No, it was later." *And why was Ellen hiding that expensive bracelet when the couple seemed to be dripping in money?*

"Didn't you say Mark is cagey about what he does? Perhaps he's selling bootleg stuff, and the law is closing in on them," said Mrs. Appleby, dramatically.

"I'm surprised you know that term, Mrs. Appleby."

"I'm not a nun in a convent you know," she replied with a cheeky grin.

"And how would the cook fit into that?" asked Percy.

Mrs. Appleby huffed. "That's true. And they could discuss their problems in the privacy of their room. No need to wander all over talking about their troubles in the kitchen."

"Ooh! That is a good point. A married couple would not need to meet in the middle of the night in the kitchen when they had all the privacy they needed in their bedrooms."

"Okay. Keep going," encouraged Mrs. Appleby.

"That leaves Walter and Phoebe Valentine. Walter is the one who lost his leg in the war."

"Yes, I remember him. Nice gentleman," said Mrs. Appleby. "A doctor, isn't he?"

Percy nodded. "But it seemed like every time I looked at him he had a whiskey in his hand. I don't remember him being a big drinker before. And, I happened upon Pheobe writing that note she claimed was for the butcher. I've never asked my butcher to meet me anywhere."

"Me neither," agreed Mrs. Appleby. "So, if it was not for the butcher, who was it really for?"

"The thought that Phoebe could be unfaithful too gives me a headache. She and Walter have always been rock solid." She moaned. "My friends are all falling apart."

"I think there are some things there that bear following up on," said Mrs. Appleby, grabbing a notepad from a drawer. "Such as, what are the Richmonds importing and whether they're in financial difficulties? And what is Phoebe up to?"

"You mean like, spy on them? Whatever for?" asked Percy.

"To give you a sense of purpose, my dear. Didn't you just tell me that now both boys are away at school you need some direction?"

"I did say that, yes, but isn't poking my nose into other people's lives rather dangerous? Especially when there has been a murder?"

"I'm not suggesting you put yourself in harm's way, Mrs. Pontefract. But you were the one who found the body. You must be a little bit curious. I'm just suggesting you socialize with your friends some more and get them talking. It is the Christmas season, after all."

Percy's whole soul rejected the crazy idea. Gumshoeing was for the police to do. Anyway, she was quite content with her lot. *Wasn't she?*

"Perhaps you could think of it as a huge riddle," continued Mrs. Appleby. "You like riddles and the daily crossword. I think you would be good at it."

Percy squeezed an eye as she pondered. It was a better idea than tennis or golf. "I don't think so," she protested, with less energy than before. "I shall be busy with the boys and Piers in the run up to Christmas."

"About that," began Mrs. Appleby.

Percy looked up.

"Mr. Pontefract called and left a message with me this morning. He won't be home until Christmas Eve."

Chapter 11

Percy's heart sank. "Are you kidding? I had so many plans of things to do with Piers and the boys."

Mrs. Appleby took a sip of her tea. "He was very apologetic but said it could not be helped."

"Did he at least tell you where he was or where I could contact him?" A feeling of loss overwhelmed her.

"He just said he would be in the Midlands. Even as he spoke to me someone was calling him to leave."

Percy could not stand the look of pity in Mrs. Appleby's eyes and began to worry a piece of dry skin hanging from her thumb.

"Another reason to take a stab at this murder mystery," said the cook. "Pun intended."

A reluctant smile tugged at Percy's mouth. "You make it sound like an Agatha Christie novel. But when you actually land on a dead body it is quite terrifying."

"I don't doubt it, lovey."

"Well, I'm going to have to entertain the boys somehow. I might as well kill two birds with one stone. I can make some arrangements to visit my friends so that the children have people to play with. I'm not saying I *will* spy on them you understand, but it might be fun for the boys."

Ellen and Mark Richmond lived in a boxy, modern monstrosity that was all windows and angles. Bartie had spent the entire journey with a face like a wet dishrag but Percy had hopes that Ellen's twelve-year-old son would prove entertaining for him. William on the other hand had whistled Christmas tunes the whole way. It was a skill he had recently learned but not yet mastered.

A long muddy driveway, edged with naked trees, led to a circular forecourt. The front door was on the second level and Percy eyed the icy steps with trepidation.

"Here Mum, hold onto me," said William offering his little elbow.

She slid a large hand through his arm and grabbed the iron railing with the other, as her bulky handbag swung from her elbow.

Ignoring the tutting sound behind her, she made it to the top without incident.

"Percy!" cried Ellen, as though they had not seen each other in months. "Philly, Edward! Your friends are here." Large diamond studs twinkled in her ears and Percy was reminded of the expensive bracelet.

Percy could have sworn she heard Bartie murmur that they were *not* his friends as they piled into the minimalist foyer and hoped Ellen had not heard. It was hard to understand how people could live in such a cold, stark environment that felt more like a morgue than a home.

"Let me take your coats," said Ellen. "Nellie! Visitors!"

A girl of about seventeen with bucked teeth and pimples hurried from the back of the house and took the coats from Ellen.

"So hard to find decent help," Ellen whispered. "Now, are you ready for tea?"

They entered a large, blank room full of steel and bold leather furniture. Percy shivered. The front wall was completely made of glass. Between two black sofas was a chrome coffee table laden with slices of cake and cream pastries. An unadorned silver tea pot stood in the middle of a tray surrounded by plain white teacups with chunky handles. Percy's mother would have had a heart attack.

"Have a seat," said Ellen as her children burst into the room. At age eight, Philly was a petite, blonde girl with teeth too big for her mouth and a button nose. She ran over to William and surrounded him in a hug, then taking his hand, led him from the room, while lisping. "You will love my dolls house. Don't worry, it has soldiers to protect the ladies."

Edward advanced on the sullen Bartie and held out a stiff hand. "I say, have you used an Erector Set?"

A long dim light went on in Bartie's eyes. This was the very item he had mentioned wanting for Christmas. "No, but I have read about them."

The two of them left the room and thundered up the bare, metal stairs.

"Well, that was quick," said Ellen with a laugh. "Tea?"

"Yes, please. Milk and two sugars."

As Ellen poured, Percy looked around the room. There was a disturbing work of modern art with triangles and eyes in odd places, a sorry looking elephant plant with red Christmas balls hanging from it, and an unexpected suit of armor.

Ellen caught her gaze. "Hideous, isn't it? Mark just *had* to have it. Cost a fortune."

"It's the kind of thing people have in stately homes," said Percy trying to find something positive to say.

"That's why I was so against it. I spent a fortune on an interior designer and the armor throws the whole thing off."

Percy took a sip of tea before she put her foot in her mouth by blurting out a joke about wasted funds.

"So, have you recovered?" Ellen asked her.

Percy frowned.

"From your escapade with the dead body?" explained Ellen. "I would have been silly for a week."

"Oh, that! I've had a bit of trouble sleeping since I got home, but the memory is fading." This was a complete lie. She had barely slept a wink since arriving home and with no Piers to cuddle up to, she spent most of the night gripping her eiderdown, staring at the ceiling in terror.

"I am glad you called. I've been wanting to explain about that bracelet." Ellen's face sank into a smile so sickly sweet it could give a person toothache.

Percy's senses stood to attention.

"It's silly really," Ellen began. "I saw it in Hatton Garden a few weeks ago and just couldn't get it out of my mind. I even mentioned it to Mark as an idea for a Christmas present. When he asked how much it was, he became very excitable and said that some of his imports had been delayed and cashflow was tight. He said he might be able to get it for my birthday in the summer but that for the time being, with Christmas coming for the children and everything, it was out of the question." She flicked a crumb from her light pink cashmere skirt. "Do *you* like diamonds, Percy?"

"I'm more of a pearl person actually," she replied, taking a second slice of banana loaf.

"Well, I'm all in for diamonds." Ellen quivered with pleasure. "It's the way they glisten in the light." Her eyes filled with hunger. "I'm obsessed." She fingered the ones in her ears. "I just had to have it. I couldn't concentrate on anything else, you know?"

Percy did not know but she nodded while chewing.

"So, I told Mark I was going to Mother's, and I actually went back to Hatton Garden and got the bracelet. He would be furious, which means I can be satisfied with owning the thing, but I daren't actually wear it. I carry it around in my handbag and look at it from time to time."

This sounded like rather odd behavior to Percy, but she decided to keep her own counsel.

"That's why I was so nervous when you saw it slip out of my bag. We already had enough on our plates with the murder. Finding out I had bought the expensive bracelet would have tipped Mark over the edge."

"You didn't have to explain anything," Percy assured her.

"Well, with police everywhere I didn't want you to mention it as suspicious or anything."

Too late!

Thinking of her conversation with Mrs. Appleby, Percy thought this might be a good opening for snooping. "What did you tell the police in your interview?"

"Not much. We were sound asleep until all the screaming and people herding down the stairs. I take a sleeping draught when I have a lot of excitement. I was extremely groggy for having been woken up in the middle of the night."

"Does Mark take it too?" asked Percy, her fingers itching for another slice. She took a sip instead.

"Oh, no! He can sleep anywhere."

"So, you can't be sure he had been in bed all night?" The minute the words were out of her mouth Percy regretted them. "I mean, if… if you sleep so soundly he…he could sleepwalk and you wouldn't know it." She tried to chortle but the sound was more like a stranded tortoise.

The sugary smile had just been infused with lemon juice. "Very funny." Ellen's hands adjusted the colorful silk scarf at her neck. "In fact, Mark had to shake me awake."

"Do you remember who you saw on the landing or stairs," asked Percy.

"Well, like I said, I was awfully woozy, but Tom was already headed to the kitchen and Bruce was halfway down. Jemima looked like she had seen a ghost, peering over the banister in a flannel dressing gown with Verity. Poor Walter was late out on his crutches—no time to strap on his leg."

"Where was Phoebe?"

Ellen closed her eyes then frowned. "I didn't see her until I was down the stairs and into the kitchen. She came in a few minutes after me. She was pale as milk too."

"Have you thought about who might have killed the cook?" asked Percy, deciding that it would be impolite not to sample the cream cakes.

"Not really. Best left to the police." Ellen clasped her hands around her knees, rings standing out from her fingers like knuckle-dusters.

"But you *do* think it was one of us?" Percy prodded, conscious that her bite had squeezed cream along her cheek.

"One of—? Oh, no!" Ellen huffed with derision. "You're my friends. Known you all for donkey's years. I'm not going to go around suspecting any of *you*. No, I'm sure the police will discover that it was an intruder." Ellen lifted a finger to point to the errant cream and Percy took a napkin and wiped her face.

"You don't suspect one of us, do you?" she asked.

Percy shrugged. "I haven't really thought about it. I prefer the idea of it being a stranger but…"

"But what?" Ellen's arms were crossed tight across her chest.

"Nothing." She lifted her cup for Ellen to refill. "Have you had a second interview?"

"The inspector is coming tomorrow. I'm dreading it. He's such a grouchy bundle of thistles." She made eye contact. "Have you?"

"Yes, but I think it's because I found the body."

Time to try another angle.

"It was the first time I had seen Verity and Tom for ages. Have you done anything with them recently?"

"We went to opening day at Wimbledon with them in June," replied Ellen. "But I hadn't seen them since then."

"I thought they seemed a bit stressed." Percy let the suggestion hang in the air.

"Stressed?"

"You know, like they were having relationship problems."

Ellen pitched forward. "What makes you say that?"

"I hate to gossip—"

"Yes?" If Ellen leaned any farther forward, she would land on the floor at Percy's feet.

Percy decided to bite the bullet. "I saw Verity in the garden with a man. It was not Tom."

Ellen's eyes grew round. "When you say *in* the garden...?"

"I mean canoodling."

Ellen's hand slammed her chest. "No!"

Percy nodded with thin lips.

"I can't believe it. Though, now that you mention it, they did seem a bit frosty when they arrived at Wimbledon. I put it down to the traffic, but it could have been something else. Trouble in Eden."

"Maybe there is a perfectly innocent explanation," suggested Percy, backpedaling.

"Well, she was hardly meeting her doctor in the garden in the cold of December, was she? And you said they were kissing. What other explanation could there be?"

"I think we should keep it between us though, don't you? Something so private," said Percy, withholding the fact that Verity had confessed to the transgression.

Disappointment clouded Ellen's pretty face. "I suppose so."

"Tell me about the cruise," said Percy, and the conversation turned to the mundane for the rest of her stay.

Chapter 12

After telling Mrs. Appleby about Ellen's diamond addiction, Percy thought it might be a good idea to investigate her other friends in their own environments before drawing too many conclusions.

But first she needed to get a tree with the boys.

Farmer Comstock had a wood full of fir trees and allowed the locals to come and chop them down for a few shillings. Digging out a handsaw from the potting shed, she loaded the boys into the car and set out.

"Let's see who can find the finest tree," she said, once they had parked. A light snow had fallen in the night, dusting the small forest with a hint of magic. But the breeze was biting sharp and she wrapped her scarf more tightly around her neck.

The boys were bundled up warm and ran like the wind to scavenge for the best tree. Percy trailed behind thinking about Ellen and her diamonds. Percy had never been fascinated by expensive jewelry like other women. She would rather spend that kind of money on a horse for the boys, if they had it. She tried to imagine how much a bracelet like the one she saw would cost and came up blank.

She had practically had to drag Bartie away from the Erector set and determined to buy him one for Christmas. At least she would be sure of hitting the nail on the head.

"Found one!" William's excitement traveled on the air and she hurried to catch up with him through the maze of narrow footpaths. She found him standing proudly by an enormous tree with wide reaching boughs. It was rather lop-sided, thick on the right but thinner on the left. But his toothy grin grabbed her heart and wouldn't let go. The only problem would be fitting it onto the car.

"Marvelous!" she cried. "But we need to take a look at Bartie's offering before we make a decision."

William clicked his heels and saluted.

"Bartie!" she called. "Bartie!"

"Over here!" he yelled back. "I have found a monster!"

Taking William's hand, they tied red ribbon around trees along their way so that they could find his again. They spotted Bartie in a small clearing by a tree even taller than William's but much more even. It was close to several smaller trees that would have got Percy's vote, but she knew that at their age, biggest equaled best.

Bartie was beaming. A real, honest, bone deep smile of triumph.

"Wow!" squealed William. "This is even better than the one I found. Don't you think so, Mummy?"

She tipped her head to see the top. She was pretty sure they would have to chop the top off to squeeze it into the living room, but the boys wouldn't care. It was finding a tree they all agreed on together that mattered. She handed Bartie the red-handled hand saw. He looked down at it and then questioned her with his hazel eyes.

"You're eleven. I think that's old enough to be responsible with a saw," she said and wished she could capture his delight in a bottle to look at during his sullen moments.

"Thank you! I won't let you down!"

He employed the tool with gusto and within ten minutes the tree began to tip. "Timber!" he cried, and William joined in as the whole tree crashed to the ground. Percy grabbed hold of the trunk and pulled. It didn't budge.

"It might take two of us," said William, gripping the end with his blue mittens.

Nothing.

"It needs a man," said Bartie with pride, flexing his arms and grabbing the trunk.

Between the three of them, they slowly dragged the tree back to the car, but Percy knew that they did not have the strength to lift it on top.

"We'll need to call on Farmer Comstock to help us," she said.

"It's alright Mummy," William reassured her. "Even Daddy needs help with this bit."

Having almost put her back out getting the large box of decorations from the converted stables, Percy was now draped with homemade garlands as the boys tried to untangle the strands. She had lopped off six inches to be able to stand the tree upright and it filled the corner of the room with its thick circumference. The scent was divine.

Once the garlands were on, the glass balls were hung and then the homemade ornaments, which were her favorites. When the tree was finished, it would not have been out of place in the grandest of Victorian homes. The boys applauded.

Satisfied with their efforts and after a scrumptious lunch, they set off for an afternoon of tobogganing at the Goodfellow's. Jemima and Bruce had recently bought an enormous house just five miles from the Pontefracts, that sat at the top of the perfect sledding hill. When Percy had called to suggest that her boys might like to visit, Jemima had jumped at the chance.

The fresh, overnight snowfall produced the perfect conditions for tobogganing and even Bartie was chattering with excitement. Their sophisticated sleds had been gifts from the Christmas before and were the best *Holborn Grangers* department store had to offer.

Standing at the top of the hill with Cordelia and Isolde, Percy situated herself on the back of William's vehicle.

"Aren't you coming down?" she asked Jemima.

"Heaven's no!" she declared, her pale cheeks chapped by the brisk breeze. "I'm sure to injure myself in the process. You should think twice about it too, Percy."

In spite of her tendency to attract catastrophe, Percy was determined to enjoy the hill with her boys. "A broken arm will be a badge of honor!" she cried as she poked William in the back and they pushed their way off the top.

The crisp, bite of the frosty air stung her lips and ears but exhilarated her spirit. "Yahoo!" she cried as they flew over the glittering snow, neck and neck with Bartie.

Just before the bottom, their sled hit a small shrub, throwing them both off the seat and onto their backs, shrieking with laughter. Bartie declared himself the winner, as the two Goodfellow girls brought up the rear on inferior models.

"You didn't tell us you were going," complained Isolde, her dark hair curled around her pretty eyes by the moisture. "I bet we'll win if you give us a fair chance."

"You're on," shouted Bartie with a wide smile, the knotty attitude shed, at least for the moment. All four children grabbed the handles of their sleds and scurried back up the hill kicking powdery snow behind them. Their enthusiasm was such that Percy was certain she would not make it up in time to join them. She chose to sit in the snow at the bottom, waving wildly.

Perched on the precipice, the children sat with eager expressions as Jemima stood to the side her arm in the air.

"Ready! Steady! Go!" she bellowed, as the children kicked themselves forward, propelled by gravity. Sprays of snowflakes shot out to the side of each sled as the boys and girls screamed with delight, bumping down the incline. Bartie hit the same shrub and toppled off as Cordelia flew past, William and Isolde hot on her tail.

"I told you we could win," cried Isolde, struggling to her feet in the slippery tracks.

"I'm going to win this time," yelled William, already halfway up the hill.

When their energy had waned, Percy joined them on their upward trek and traveled down with William several more times, guffawing all the way down.

"Do you want to come on my sled," asked Bartie after half an hour. Percy almost tripped over her boots with surprise and delight.

They won the race but caught an edge at the bottom and rolled off, crying with laughter that made her stomach hurt. She lay exhausted on her back, feeling the true joy of parenthood and tipped her head to the side. Bartie was smiling at her. Gone was the ruffled hedgehog that her son had become at school. Returned to her was the pure, innocent child of her heart and she felt her eyes swimming.

When their calf muscles could take it no more, and they had worn the snow through to the grass, they all trudged back to the house. They cast off their coats, gloves, and boots like snakes shedding their skin, and padded through to the sitting room where the housekeeper brought them hot tea and cocoa. When their thirst was quenched and their hunger satisfied, the children left to go to the playroom that had once been a nursery, leaving Jemima and Percy alone.

"Don't you wish you had joined in?" Percy asked her.

"I had plenty of fun watching all of you." Jemima placed her teacup on the table.

"This is such a lovely place," Percy said, popping a cream puff into her mouth. "It's my first time here. How on earth do you afford a housekeeper and so many maids?"

"An unmarried uncle died in South America last year and left his entire estate to Bruce. It was quite a fortune and Bruce wanted to sink it in to land. He also got promoted at work, so that was nice."

"How many staff do you keep?" asked Percy.

"We have a cook, a kitchen maid, two house maids, a full-time gardener, a groom and of course, the housekeeper."

Percy tried to stop her eyes popping out of her head. "Heavens! Those are pre-war numbers."

"I know!" acknowledged Jemima. "I feel so fortunate."

The grand Georgian house was at least two hundred years old but not in the least draughty, which meant the Goodfellows had sunk a lot of money into improvements. The walls were all paneled in rich, carved oak, and the shining parquet floors covered with plush Persian rugs in reds and greens. Though the vaulted room was large, it was warm and toasty.

"I haven't a clue what Piers does for his job. He's very vague about it. Is that how Bruce is?" she asked.

"He says he doesn't want to bore me with the details," replied Jemima. "But he's home more than Piers appears to be. Do you find it lonely?"

Percy huffed. "I do! Especially when the boys are at school. I'm looking for a hobby to fill my days. I thought I might try my hand at sl—spelunking, but it's not encouraged in the winter." She had almost let slip her true hobby and only quick thinking had saved her. She wasn't even sure what spelunking was.

"Exploring caves?" Jemima's head reared back. "I think you should choose something a little less dangerous and closer to home," said Jemima.

Oh, caves.

"What do *you* do for fun?" Percy asked.

A golden Labrador had nosed its way into the room and come to lay by the fire. Percy wiggled her stockinged toes into his back as he grunted with pleasure.

When no response was forthcoming, she turned to her friend. "Jemima?"

"I suppose I read a lot," she said. "Not the stuffy tomes we inherited with the house, you understand. I prefer

73

romance novels." She said this as though it were the eighth deadly sin.

"What's wrong with that?" asked Percy.

"Bruce thinks they're trashy. At his urging I'm trying to join the bridge club in the village. But the others in the group are Lady this and Lady that. I'm afraid they would look down on me and my guilty pleasure as lowbrow."

"Nonsense! If they're worth knowing they wouldn't be such snobs," remarked Percy. "Do you even like bridge?" Her mother was a member of a bridge club which was the only qualification against it that Percy needed, frankly.

"Bruce says it's important to dig roots into the community and that the bridge club is the way in."

Since when was Bruce so interested in status? She was reminded of the diamond cufflinks. An influx of funds had given him airs, it appeared.

"There must be other ways like charity boards and such," suggested Percy. A bridge club would be nothing short of a punishment.

"There's the policeman's ball which raises money for charity," said Jemima. "But Bruce insists on the bridge thing."

Since Jemima had opened the door, Percy thought she would walk through it since that was the real reason they had come today.

"What did you think of the policeman who came to the Howard's place? He acted like he had pinecones in his underwear all the time."

Jemima's fragile face transformed from anxiety to amusement. She put down her cup, held her belly and laughed for a full minute.

"Oh, Percy! You do have a way with words. That is the perfect description of the acerbic man. His interview felt more like an inquisition."

"Spot on! I thought it was just me. He basically said that since I was the last one to see the cook, I was the number one suspect," revealed Percy.

"He did not! I always thought it was the last person to see the victim *alive* who was the prime suspect," retorted Jemima offering Percy the plate of fairy cakes.

Percy took one with colorful sprinkles atop soft, white icing. "That's right! I was too nervous to think straight. I tripped and fell out of his office like I was drunk. I'm sure he has a low opinion of me."

Jemima chuckled as she took a cake with glazed orange slices on top. "He asked me if Bruce and I were in our rooms all night. I said yes, but Bruce *did* go to the bathroom."

Percy was all ears. "Me too. We had all drunk so much." She took a small bite of cake. "What time was that?"

"Around half past two. I stirred when he returned."

"I heard the floorboards creak and a door close when I used the facilities before heading down to the kitchen," said Percy. "I must have just missed him in the hall. Does he often get up in the night?"

Jemima's eyes rolled upward in thought. "No. But as you pointed out, we did drink a great deal during the festivities."

"Yes, we did," Percy agreed.

"There's one other thing that has been bothering me," Jemima said in a quiet voice, scooting forward in her chair.

Percy leaned her large frame forward and quietly waited.

"We had quite forgotten, but Mrs. Barlow was my mother-in-law's cook for a brief time before the war."

"That's an incredible coincidence, isn't it?" asked Percy. "Why did she let her go?"

"Some of the silver went missing, and it was found tucked in Mrs. Barlow's drawer, hidden."

"How on earth did she get a good reference?" asked Percy.

"His mother was not one hundred percent sure it was her. Mrs. Barlow denied that she had done it and claimed she had been framed, but someone had to pay. So, the compromise was that she would be let go but her reference would make no mention of the theft."

"Did you disclose this connection to the inspector?"

"No. We didn't realize it until later, and it didn't seem relevant. Do you think we should?" Jemima's face was pinched with worry.

"Have you had a second interview?" asked Percy. "You'd better mention it then, in case it looks like you're hiding something."

"The inspector is coming over tomorrow evening when Bruce is home. I can tell him then."

On the drive back, the boys fell asleep, but Percy's mind was busy. *Was it Bruce in the hallway that night? And was it relevant that he had an undisclosed connection to the cook?*

Chapter 13

The last couple on the list of possible suspects were Phoebe and Walter. They lived in Hampshire, the next county over. Percy had suggested building snowmen, but the snow had melted overnight and after a quick change of plans, Phoebe had proposed riding. The Valentine's owned several horses, plenty for all the children to ride.

Phoebe and Walter had three children, the youngest being a happy-go-lucky three-year-old who peered out from behind his mother's legs with a playful grin. All four of them and several dogs, answered the door and the two older children immediately absconded with William and Bartholomew who had retained his brighter self.

"Come in, come in!" Phoebe's tone was bright, cheerful, and welcoming.

Their home was a traditional red brick square with pleasingly symmetrical windows around a blue front door. The inside smelled of fruit cake and apples.

Phoebe swept the toddler up into her arms, as comfortable with a snotty nosed child as with her friends. So many of Percy's acquaintances hired nannies for their young children and hardly saw their offspring. Percy could not understand it and felt a kinship to Phoebe as she slung the child onto her hip and beckoned for Percy to follow her down the paneled hall to a snug room with dark red walls and a hearty fire.

The red velvet brocade furniture trimmed with gold piping was slightly shabby but incredibly comfortable and Percy sunk into it with pleasure. Phoebe took a well-loved armchair and snuggled the child into her arms, kissing the top of his head.

"How are you doing?" Phoebe asked.

"What do you mean?" responded Percy.

"You know. After your shock. I would be a blubbering mess still." She laid a smooth cheek against the little boy's head.

"Oh! That. I must admit I have trouble sleeping," Percy confessed.

"Veronal. If I'm up with the baby and can't get back to sleep, I use it. Marvelous stuff."

"It's not that bad," Percy replied. She had never once thought to take a sleeping aid.

"Wasn't that inspector awful?" Phoebe continued. "Got out of the wrong side of the bed, if you ask me." The child stuck a dirty thumb in his mouth and stared unabashedly at Percy with clear blue eyes.

"Perhaps the problem was that he never actually got to bed that night," responded Percy.

"Yes, that *would* make someone rather grouchy. But he should have dug into his reserve of civility. Shockingly ill mannered."

Percy couldn't help but agree. The inspector had made no friends.

"Will you be going to the funeral?" Phoebe asked her.

"I suppose so." She had received an invitation that morning with a note begging her to come since Mrs. Barlow had no family and few friends.

"I might try to get out of it," said Phoebe, hugging the small boy on her lap. "I didn't even know the woman and to have to leave the children all day again…"

"I quite understand," replied Percy. "I don't really want to go, but I don't have a ready excuse. Hopefully, we can be in and out quickly. Pay our respects and be off."

The dogs lifted their heads then ran for the hall, barking their heads off. The door to the pleasant room burst open and Walter appeared looking uptight.

"They sent me—" He noticed Percy and stopped. "They sent me a bottle of wine."

"Who?" asked Phoebe, her jaw strained.

78

"Some grateful patients. Hello, Percy. I forgot you were coming." He shuffled over and kissed his wife and child. "Where is everyone else?" he asked, his chiseled face showing signs of fatigue.

"In the playroom." Her casual tone had become much more guarded.

"Ah, yes. Well, I'll leave you to it, then," he said, and promptly left the room.

"Does he not have to be in surgery today?" asked Percy, after he had disappeared.

"He has the afternoon off," said Phoebe, her eyes lingering on the door. "Shall we saddle up?"

Both Percy's boys were very comfortable on a horse. The energetic animals were already saddled when they went to the stables on the side of the house. Each of the Valentine's older children had their own ponies which left one full-size mare and two smaller animals.

"Can I ride this one?" giggled William, looking up at a chestnut pony who was trying to nibble his ear.

"Of course!" said Phoebe with her casual charm returned. "It looks like he may have already chosen you!"

Bartie mounted a beautiful calico, beaming from ear to ear. He was a sort of horse-whisperer, and Percy wished they had the funds to buy him one of his own. There was an affinity between him and the animals that was almost mystical. Seeing him so content, she wondered if it was the school making him miserable.

Phoebe, holding hands with her toddler, led her other children on their horses out to an enclosed field, and Percy led her own boys out. They closed the gate and leaned against the split rail fence, as their children rode the horses around the space. Billowing white plumes burst from their active mouths in the frosty air as they bumped up and down in the saddles and for some time, Percy was caught up in total bliss, forgetting there had been a murder.

Bartie gently kicked his mount's flanks and the beautiful beast began to trot, throwing him higher in the saddle. William was content to walk his horse and chat with Phoebe's children. He waved at Percy each time he went by, as if he had not seen her in years. Her heart blossomed under her heavy coat. Why couldn't they go to school near home and be day boys? Piers always said that it was tradition; the boys should go to the school he, his father, and his grandfather had attended. He also maintained it made men of them. It was a cursed tradition in her opinion. They were still little boys. She determined to bring up the thorny topic over Christmas.

"Bartie is quite the horseman, isn't he?" commented Phoebe.

"He is. Took to horses before his second birthday."

"Can't you get him his own?"

Percy took a deep breath. "We're stretched pretty thin, as it is. But Jemima told me that Bruce got a raise, so I shall cross my fingers for that since he and Piers are in the same profession."

"Horses *are* expensive," Phoebe agreed. "I sometimes wonder if we'll be able to keep all ours."

Percy turned to her. "Really? I thought surgeons were paid pretty well."

"Oh, they are. But that's how expensive the horses are to keep."

Percy turned back to watch her boys. If it was too expensive for the Valentines, then she would have to be content with her children riding other people's horses.

Back in the house for tea, they made a merry crowd all sitting around the little table indulging in the pastries and cakes. The children had worked up an appetite and were stuffing their mouths while telling jokes. Percy had not felt so content in a long time and didn't want the day to end.

When all the cakes had vanished, Percy looked at the clock. It was five and darkness was falling. She hated to drive at night.

"Perhaps we should get going," she began.

"No! Mum, no," cried Bartie. "We have a game of war to finish upstairs. *Please* let's stay."

Given how rare it was these days for Bartie to be excited about anything, she relented. It was already dark. It wasn't like she could take a brush and paint the light back into the sky.

"Alright. One more hour but we need to be back by seven for dinner otherwise Mrs. Appleby will be very cross."

Bartie saluted with a grin and all four of them ran out of the room and roared up the stairs, the toddler trailing behind them.

"Watch Markus!" shouted Phoebe after them, laughing. "What was life before children?"

"I agree. They are my reason for living," said Percy.

Phoebe clasped her hands to her face and looked at Percy over her knuckles. "Did you think it would be this amazing?"

"To be honest, I thought I was going to be the most horrible mother," she began. "But as soon as Bartie was born, it was like someone had waved a magic wand and endowed me with maternal power."

"I always wanted children," said Phoebe. "I spent more time in the nurseries when we visited other people than with children my own age. I have not been disappointed."

For the next hour they talked of their children, their funny escapades and childish phrases and when the clock struck six, Percy was surprised and reluctant to leave.

"I'll go and get them," said Phoebe, pulling her enviable figure from the chair.

Percy went in search of their coats and boots as the children clattered down the wooden stairs, complaining about having to leave. Bundling her boys into their warm outerwear, she opened the door as the children still chatted and laughed, tumbling down the steps in the dark and into the car.

As Percy turned to say goodbye, a necklace on Phoebe's young daughter winked in the porch light. A red crystal necklace with one stone missing. The stone that was sitting at the bottom of her capacious bag.

Chapter 14

A heavy gray sky, waiting for a celestial signal to dump its load of snow, frowned on the funeral below. Percy's fur-lined boots were failing miserably in their job as she stood elbow to elbow with Jemima in the frigid church, casting worried glances outside at the weather. Since Piers had disappeared, and the forecast was not good, she had decided to take a taxi to the funeral of the Howard's cook, but she was increasingly concerned that she would be marooned in Hampstead by the inevitable blizzard.

She wiggled numb toes, rocking from side to side to induce her circulation but it was no good. Her fingers were not faring much better, and she had already dropped the hymnbook twice.

Almost everyone from the lethal Christmas party was present, everyone except Mark Richmond and Bruce Goodfellow. As anticipated, there were no family members present and only a few older ladies from the village. In spite of the inconvenience, Percy was glad she had made the effort.

A gleaming oak coffin, blanketed with complicated floral arrangements, stood at the front of the church. Physical evidence of the Howard's generosity—or could it be a sign of assuaging guilt?

The toneless vicar indicated for them to rise and sing another hymn. Rather than inspire the soul, the few untrained voices present, rattled and echoed around the stone walls like the squawking of angry birds. It made Percy want to cry for the unheralded woman in the casket. Funerals did force one to reflect on one's own mortality. Would a showing at her service be any better? Would Piers even be able to make time for it? She swatted the negative thought away. He was a good man, dedicated to his career. It could be worse.

As the vicar raised the final prayer with the dramatic intonation of the clergy, the few mourners stood and watched the pall bearers carry the coffin out to the graveyard.

"How bally awful was that?" sniffed Phoebe who fell into step beside them. "Strangers pretending to mourn you."

They plodded up the aisle in the wake of the casket and stepped outside just as the skies could no longer hold their chilly burden. Percy was glad of the huge Russian fur hat she had worn with its dual purpose of covering her insubordinate curls and keeping her dry. Flakes as big as pennies fell softly, covering the ground and the coffin within minutes.

"Ashes to ashes..." droned the vicar.

Howard and Verity stepped forward to throw soil on the casket.

"Dust to dust..."

Jemima swallowed down a sob.

"I thought you didn't know Mrs. Barlow well," Percy commented.

"It's not her," sniffled her friend. "It's Bruce."

Percy's stomach dropped.

"He's been acting rather strange," she whimpered.

"Strange how?" whispered Percy.

"Though after my skin, worms destroy this body..."

Jemima's skin furrowed like ripples from a stone in a lake.

"He has started reading a great deal."

Percy was tempted to chuckle until she caught the stink eye of the vicar and coughed it away.

"Reading? That's not so strange," she reasoned.

"But Bruce *hates* reading. Something is wrong, I just know it."

As soon as the vicar said 'amen', the little old ladies from the village made a mad dash to get home before the snow got too deep. Percy could not blame them.

"Have you tried talking to him about it?" she asked Jemima.

"He's always too busy or waves me away." Jemima took out a large man's handkerchief and blew her little nose like a trumpet as snow fell from her hat like a veil in front of her face.

Tom crunched over, the snow now a half inch thick. "Back to our house for a bite?" Though it was framed as a question, it was not a question. Percy was becoming concerned that she would be stranded again. Much as she liked her friends, staying over with them again was not in her plans.

"Of course," she said, plastering on a fake smile.

"You can both fit in our car," Tom assured them.

The snow was getting thicker by the minute. Tom had to scrape a layer off the windscreen before he could see anything.

"Wasn't that nice?" boomed Verity as Percy squeezed her big bottom into the tiny seat behind the front passenger and pulled her knees up to her considerable chest.

"Mmm," was all she could manage and be truthful.

"Did *you* find it moving, Jemima?" asked Verity, staring at the clearly emotional Jemima in the rearview mirror

Panicked eyes locked with Percy's. "Oh, yes," she murmured. "Very touching."

A blast of snow blew in on the three of them as Tom opened his door and Percy gritted her teeth against the cold as several flakes melted on her nose.

"Just as well we don't have far to go," Tom said, inching away from the curb at a steady three miles per hour.

Percy looked out the back window to see the distinct tracks left by the narrow tires. If this storm didn't break soon, the snow would drift and no traffic would venture out, not even taxis.

Although the Howard's house was only a mile away from the church, it took fifteen minutes to crawl there. Once they parked, all three passengers hurried into the house as the second car, driven by Walter, pulled in behind them holding Phoebe, and Ellen.

The blast of warmth from the large fire in the sitting room was like a welcoming hug and having stripped off her outer clothes, Percy went to embrace the hearth, rubbing her hands up and down her arms.

"Who wants a brandy?" asked Verity. "That will warm us from the inside out."

Several hands shot into the air including the doctor's. Percy caught a fleeting look of scorn shadow Phoebe's refined features.

"We've ordered some sandwiches from the bakery that were delivered while we were gone," Verity explained. "As soon as we warm up, we can go on through."

"Are you going to replace the cook?" asked Jemima.

"Not in the immediate future. We hope Martha will grow into the job," said Verity, suddenly busying herself with sweeping the ashes from the hearth. The Howards of last year would have already hired a new cook. What had changed?

The sandwiches were made from fresh cottage loaves and Percy realized it had been hours since breakfast. She filled her plate until it was groaning with bread, pickled onions, beets, and cheese. Spotting a seat open at the table, she sat down by Ellen who had made no attempt to get any of the food.

"Not hungry?" asked Percy, hand poised over her meal.

Ellen's jaw strained as she gripped her stomach. "Not really."

"I say, is something wrong," whispered Percy. "Did Mark find out about the bracelet?"

A fan of lines fluttered between Ellen's eyes as her hand covered her mouth. "Oh, Percy! The bracelet is the least of my worries."

Eyeing a round, golden onion, Percy resisted the urge to pop it in her mouth at the very moment a friend was about to bare her soul. Crunching pickles did not align well with sympathetic listening.

"Whatever do you mean?"

Ellen checked to make sure no one else was listening. "Mark has disappeared."

"So has Piers," Percy said with warmth.

"No. I mean *really* gone. He did not come home two nights ago, and I have not been able to reach him. None of his colleagues seem to know where he is either." She leaned in closer to Percy's ear. "I think something bad may have happened."

Percy felt a jolt. "Have you called the police?"

Ellen's distraught expression transformed to the shame of a child caught stealing sweet pie from the kitchen. "I daren't. I don't think all of my husband's business dealings over the last year have been exactly…legal."

Percy dropped her sandwich, knocking over her wine glass and spilling the dark red contents all over the white cloth.

"Oh, Percy!" cried Verity. "Could we not get through one meal where you don't spill something."

Percy shot up, blotting the spill with her napkin, spewing apologies.

Once everyone's attention was back to their own conversations, Percy asked Ellen, "Do you know what he's into?"

"He told me it was better not to ask him questions. We used to import silks and silk articles from China along with jade but people have lost a taste for that, so he had to divest. Honestly, I don't really know what he's trading in these days. All I know is that the money is drying up fast."

She took a long drink of wine. "I'm worried sick that he's lying hurt in a gutter somewhere…or worse. Otherwise, I know he would have tried to contact me."

Tom knocked his glass with a spoon to get everyone's attention. "I'd just like to thank you all for coming today and propose that we raise our glasses to Mrs. Barlow." There was a pallor to his complexion that had seeped into his skin the day after the murder.

"Mrs. Barlow," everyone parroted.

Percy looked around the table. She knew so much more about her friends now, and like Pandora's infamous box, she could not stuff that knowledge back in and pretend she didn't. Verity and Tom on the rocks, Mark missing amidst serious financial worries and dodgy trade practices, finding Phoebe's missing red crystal in the kitchen *after* the murder, and Jemima's concerns about changes in her husband's habits.

She picked up her glass and took a slug. Could any of these issues be connected to the murder?

Snow was falling thick and fast outside the window and a glance at her watch showed that it was already half past three. Darkness would descend within the hour.

As she was about to ask to use the telephone to call a taxi, their meal was interrupted by a heavy pounding on the front door. Verity went to open it and a muffled, urgent male voice trickled under the door. The guests looked at each other with unease.

"It's Mr. Phillips, the gardener," said Verity coming to the door. "He says that the local police have been by to say that there is so much snow, no vehicles are allowed on the roads."

"But I have to get back," griped Walter. "I have an important meeting in the morning."

"That won't be possible," said the tall man in the bulky wool coat, pushing his way into the room.

Percy dropped her sandwich a second time. It was the ardent man from the shed.

Chapter 14

Something passed between Verity and Howard but it was not an accusation, rather concern that they would be called upon to house everyone again.

Verity went out into the hall with the gardener as Howard's gaze lingered after her. *He knows.* The conversation at the table erupted in distress at being stranded away from home a second time. Percy had promised the boys a day of skating tomorrow at Potter's Pond, if the ice was thick enough. However, as she was about to go into the hall to ring Mrs. Appleby, the contraption shrieked like an angry housewife.

"I'll get that," said Howard, leaping from his chair.

The lunch guests continued to complain about their forced stay at the house when Howard returned, his face even more strained than when he left.

"Ellen, the call is for you."

The table went silent as Ellen's expression slid from annoyance to panic.

Fearing bad news, Percy asked, "Would you like me to come with you?"

Ellen nodded and Percy trailed after her.

The earpiece was resting on the oak telephone table and Ellen was looking at it like she might a poised cobra.

"It could be your maid calling to ask something about the children," Percy suggested.

Ellen raised distraught eyes.

"Best to get it over with," Percy encouraged.

"Mrs. Richmond speaking." Her tone was flat, thick with dread.

All Percy could hear was what sounded like squawking but when Ellen cried, "No!" and began to sink at the knees, Percy caught her and the earpiece.

"This is Mrs. Pontefract," she began, heart pounding. "I am a close friend of Mrs. Richmond. Your intelligence appears to have overpowered her."

"Frankly, I'm not surprised, madam." The voice was younger than she had expected with a heavy country accent. "This is Inspector Creed of the Kent County police. I'm afraid we have found a body we suspect to be Mr. Mark Richmond. Pulled from the river this morning. We would normally have done this in person but on arriving at the Richmond residence, we were informed that Mrs. Richmond was attending a funeral. I also understand you are snowed in."

The word 'body' had entered Percy's mind and taken up residence so that the rest of the policeman's utterances were erased from memory. She had believed Ellen's worries to be the inflated concerns of a rich woman with too much time on her hands.

"I'm sorry, Inspector," she interrupted. "Did you say 'body'?"

Ellen whimpered, shaking like a frightened puppy.

"I did. We would like Mrs. Richmond to come in to identify her husband but the current weather conditions make that impossible, obviously. He will be kept in the morgue until she can make it in."

Of all the things Percy could have imagined, having to identify one's husband, the father of your children, was among the worst.

Percy was about to end the conversation when a thought struck her. "What makes you sure it is Mark?"

"We found some identification in his inner pocket. The ink was smudged but we could just make out the name. Please offer Mrs. Richmond my condolences."

"Will do, Inspector."

She replaced the earpiece in slow motion. Ellen's face was wet with tears.

"I can't..." Ellen mumbled. "I can't."

Percy understood her to mean she could not face the people in the dining room and took her to Howard's office, sitting her in the club chair by the fire.

She waited as Ellen's tears petered out.

"I wasn't entirely honest with you," Ellen began in a watery voice. "Though I don't know the exact nature of Mark's imports, I do know that he borrowed a large sum of money from some nasty people and was not able to pay it back in time. And now they have…" She collapsed into tears again.

"There, there," said Percy awkwardly patting her shoulder.

"What will I do?" Ellen moaned. "I can't possibly pay the children's school fees, and I'll lose the house."

"Can you go home to your parents?"

Ellen looked up. Percy had the thought that Jacob Marley could not have looked more miserable.

"Have you met my mother?" Ellen croaked.

It was the one thing on which Ellen and Percy could truly commiserate—awful mothers.

"Is it not better than being homeless?" Percy asked.

Ellen groaned. "Not really."

A vision of her own difficult parent sprung to mind. Having to crawl back under the parental roof would be like swallowing a whole bottle of cod liver oil, but if it meant her children had a softer landing, she would do it. "Think of the children."

Another wave of tears erupted as Percy looked on.

Having installed Ellen in the bedroom she had occupied the night of the party, Percy headed toward the stairs. The floor squeaked under her feet and she halted. Who had been up the night of the murder? She took a step back and looked down the corridor. She had also heard a door close. Was it someone leaving their room or returning? The closest room to the bathroom was the one occupied by Bruce and Jemima. Hadn't Jemima admitted that Bruce had left their room during the night? And now Percy knew that he and Jemima had a connection to the cook.

Should she mention all this to the police? Did she have any proof? You could hardly accuse a man of murder for simply going to the toilet in the night. No. She would need to do some more investigating before making any wild accusations. *And that giggle.* Now that she had reflected on it extensively and discussed it with Mrs. Appleby, she knew it was definitely feminine. But how did that help? She sighed. She made a poor Hercule Poirot.

When Percy entered the drawing room, they all telegraphed questions through their expressions but were too polite to ask outright.

"I'm afraid the police think Mark may have drowned."

Jemima dropped her magazine. "Do you mean he's…" As though the word were dirty, she could not utter it.

"I'm afraid so. The police were calling to ask Ellen to come and identify the body as soon as she can."

"I can't believe it!" gasped Verity. "Do they think this is connected with our"—she dropped her voice as if whispering made the word less caustic—"murder?"

To be honest, Percy had made no such connection, but two deaths *was* highly suspect. The first had undoubtedly been committed by someone in the house the night of the party. Could that person be guilty of the second death? Reasoning that discussing possible theories with a murderer in the room could prove dangerous, she took a moment to choose her words carefully. Best not to alarm the killer.

She pulled her mobile face down into a deep frown. "I don't know for certain, but the inspector didn't mention the murder of Mrs. Barlow. And Mark was found in a river in Kent, miles from here." She felt an urgent impulse to leave Hampstead and find comfort and safety in front of her own fire. But a glimpse out of the window was enough to end

93

that fantasy. The heavy falling snow made a thick, moving curtain beyond the glass. They were all going nowhere fast.

"Should I go up to Ellen?" asked Verity. "See how she is?"

"I think she just wants to be alone," said Percy, now casting everyone in the room as a double murderer and withdrawing to a corner of the space with a book she had no intention of reading.

Chapter 15

After twenty minutes, Percy could stand pretending to read no more and decided to reacquaint herself with the kitchen maid by helping with dinner preparations. But there was no helping poor Martha this time around. No partridges hung hidden in the back of the larder; no fresh vegetables lay in the baskets. They would have to rustle something up out of cans and bottled summer harvest.

"Can you do anything with corned beef?" Percy asked her from the pantry, eyeing at least ten cans of the horrible stuff.

"Oh, yes!" she declared. "I grew up on corned beef. I can fry it, boil it and make it into sandwich filling."

None of those sounded remotely tasty to Percy but necessity was a hard master. "Perhaps fried then," she said. "We can have it with tinned tomato soup and pickled eggs." Not the feast of kings but it would keep the hunger pangs away.

Excusing herself, she went to put in another difficult call to Mrs. Appleby.

"Be careful, Mrs. Pontefract," she said, sounding like a witch handing down a curse. "I don't like the thought of you there with a murderer."

Thanks for the reminder.

"I shall only be alone in my bedroom and there is a lock. I trust the snow will clear tomorrow and I'll be home as soon as I can. Remind the boys about our skating trip."

Everything had set her nerves on edge and rather than go back to her friends, she decided to take a nap.

It was hard to describe the mood around the dinner table that night. A seance for the dead would have been more lively. The Howards had run out of wine—at least that's what they said—so the party was stone cold sober while trying to choke down the fried corned beef. Not a good combination. Percy tried not to notice people pushing the so-called meat around their plates and hiding it under smashed pickled eggs. Only the thin soup seemed palatable.

The snow was relentless. At least three inches had dropped while she had been napping. After the indigestible supper, Tom put the radio on, and the news broadcaster announced that it was the worst snowstorm in fifty years. If it didn't stop soon, the police would find a house full of staged skeletons.

Ellen had not come down at all and Percy hoped she had fallen asleep for the night. There were half-hearted efforts to play cards and the ever-present jigsaw which, frankly, Percy wanted to tip into the fire, but mostly there was a growing tension that could be cut by a knife.

When the clock struck nine, she jumped up with a relief greater than Houdini unlocking his infamous padlocks and announced that she was going to have an early night. Several other guests joined her, eyeing each other with suspicion up the stairs.

Locking the door, she crawled into bed fully clothed, having not brought an overnight case this time. She pulled the eiderdown up to her neck and stared at the ceiling.

Every five minutes she looked at the clock.

A scratching at the door abruptly shot Percy from a sleep she hadn't realized she'd surrendered too. Her blood stream flooded with liquid panic. Someone was trying to get into her room!

She attempted to scream but undiluted fright had rendered her mute.

Pulling the covers up to her quivering nose, Percy's brain went into overload, trying to come up with methods to attack and neutralize the terrifying intruder. A creak relayed that the door had been opened and just as she was about to fling the eiderdown over the invader and rugby tackle them to the floor while screaming at the top of her lungs, a tiny voice said,

"Percy. Are you awake?"

Ellen!

In an acid whisper Percy spat, "I thought you were the killer coming to murder me in my bed! I could have hurt you."

"I'm sorry. I was just scared," whimpered Ellen on the verge of tears again.

"How in Hades did you get into my room? I locked it!" Percy was lathering herself into a fit.

"I used my key. I think the locks are all the same."

Great! Sitting bally ducks!

Percy put on the night light and reared back at the sight of Ellen. Frankenstein had lighter shadows under his eyes.

"Quick! Come in and let's put the chair under the doorhandle," she commanded, slipping out from under the covers and pulling Ellen by the arm.

She pushed trembling hands through her unruly frizz as her blood pressure spluttered its way back to normal. Ellen sat on the edge of Percy's bed, head hanging low.

"I don't think I can go on without Mark," she wailed.

"Nonsense!" cried Percy. "You *have* to go on for the children."

Wiping her nose with a lacy handkerchief, Ellen moaned. "If they killed Mark for not paying the money he owes, they may come and kill me if I don't give it to them. I don't have it! I'd rather take myself out than have those thugs do it."

"Now, now," warned Percy. "Let's not be rash. Couldn't you sell the house and raise the funds."

"It's mortgaged," Ellen admitted.

Percy shook her head in disbelief. "You are in a pickle."

"Will you come with me?" Ellen asked.

"To your home—?"

"To identify Mark's body."

Percy took a big gulp. She had only seen one dead body up close and it was enough to last her a lifetime.

"Well..." she managed.

"Oh, please. I just can't bear it," pleaded Ellen, grabbing Percy's wrists.

She tried to feel flattered that of all the women in the house, Ellen had chosen her, but she couldn't even squeeze out one drop of appreciation. And Ellen was pinching her skin. She was going to have a long talk with Piers about his disappearing acts.

"Alright. But who knows when we're going to get out of here?" she pointed out.

"I haven't even looked outside. Is it bad?" Ellen asked. She pushed back the curtains and in the glow of the moon the snow laden grass glowed. "It's stopped snowing at least." But there were four or more inches lining the window ledge.

"Well, that's encouraging." Percy rolled onto her side, the blankets up to her ears. "I'm going to try to go back to sleep." Although the constant pulse in her ears declared otherwise.

"Oh, I'll just curl up in this chair then," said Ellen.

"Don't be silly. We can top and tail it," said Percy getting up to pull the bedding out from the bottom of the bed. "It's a double and you are tiny."

After accidentally touching feet which made Percy want to gag, they settled on opposite sides of the bed.

Still plagued by the idea that this second death might be related to the first, Percy asked into the darkness, "Ellen, do you believe that Mark was in the room with you until I started screaming, the night of Mrs. Barlow's murder?"

"I know he was," Ellen responded. "I lied to you and the police because I didn't want them checking into our business. I usually take a sleeping pill but that night we were still up. He had a lot to get off his chest about his dodgy dealings that were all coming to a head. He was telling me where he had money stashed if he needed to disappear. He told me that he'd had a will written up and laid out the contingency plans. I was so angry with him! How dare he put us all in that position. It gave me the willies and we were still up talking when we heard the screaming."

"So, the news of his death isn't a complete shock to you?" Percy pushed up on her elbow.

"Part of me thought he was over-reacting. I *never* thought it would come to this," whispered Ellen.

"And what were the contingency plans?"

"Like you said, to leave and go to my mother's."

"What about the stashed money? Perhaps you could use it to buy something up north." It would be best to put some distance between Ellen and the gangsters and land was much less expensive the farther north from London one traveled.

"It's not very much. Definitely not sufficient to buy a house. It's just enough to get by for a while."

After this somber confession, Percy was even more wide awake, her mind churning.

"Did you hear anything outside your door, that night, while you were talking?" Percy asked.

"I did hear someone chuckle. It was the kind of sound you make when you're flirting with someone, but I didn't think much of it at the time. I was reeling from Mark's confession."

Percy didn't think she had ever flirted like that in her life, but her thoughts veered to Verity and the roguish gardener. Would he have been so daring as to come into the house in the middle of the night? Had the cook surprised the pair causing them to kill her to keep their secret?

"I was so worried sick about what Mark was telling me that it didn't really register," continued Ellen. "Though I

99

did think it odd so late at night." Ellen's voice wobbled. "And now Mark's fears have come to pass." She started sobbing again and Percy hoped things would look better in the morning.

Chapter 16

A large grunting mouse was threatening to eat Percy's breakfast, its black eyes staring her down, pointed nose twitching, daring her to prevent his theft.

"Uggh!" The loud exclamation dragged Percy from her sleep to reveal that the grunting was actually coming from the end of her bed. "Your feet are in my face!" complained Ellen, lifting herself up on to her arms.

Well, at least they were both alive.

"I'm terribly sorry," Percy apologized. "My feet are rather large."

"You can say that again!" exclaimed Ellen. "What size are you?"

"A lady's size twelve," she admitted. "I have to have shoes made specially. It's frightfully expensive." She swung her offensive hooves out of the bed and padded over to the window. The snow had not started again in the night and was melting at a rapid rate.

"The barometer has swung back in our favor," she told Ellen. "I think we'll be able to leave after breakfast. If there is any, that is."

Ellen grabbed her stomach and Percy remembered that the poor woman had not eaten since lunchtime. "What do you mean by that?"

"The Howard's cupboard is rather bare," she explained. "Perhaps we can get a taxi together and make a quick stop at a bakery."

After a welcome meal of warm Danish pastries, she and Ellen had separated with plans to meet at the Kent county coroner's office that afternoon.

"You're leaving again?" whined William when she returned home, as Bartie lifted his chin, pretending not to care.

Percy cupped William's adorable, pointed chin in her hand. "Something unfortunate may have happened to Mrs. Richmond's husband, and she needs a friend's support. If your friend was afraid and asked you to help, wouldn't you do it?"

"I suppose so," he sighed. "What time will you be back?"

"I'm not sure but I expect to return before dinner," she said, hoping very much that she would. The idea of seeing another dead body was messing with her insides.

To make up for having to leave again so soon, she played a board game with them until it was time to go. Both boys followed her to the door and she gave William a paralyzing hug. Eyeing Bartie, she decided a friendly thump on the arm might go down better.

"I'll hurry home," she promised, praying that the weather would hold.

Ellen was waiting for her inside the main doors of the coroner's office, looking like a sheep ready for the slaughter. Percy went up to the reception desk to explain who they were and within minutes a man in a white coat came to greet them. She thanked heaven that his lab coat was not stained with blood. Ellen stood rooted to the spot and Percy had to pull her to follow the medical examiner.

The nauseating smell of formaldehyde clung to every surface of the dismal, gray room, in the center of which stood a table, holding a body that was covered with a blue sheet. Percy felt her legs turn to jelly.

"This way Mrs. Richmond," said the coroner, beckoning both of them forward.

Percy did not trust herself to speak in case she vomited.

As she swallowed hard, several things happened at once. The medical examiner pulled back the sheet and Ellen

102

screamed and fell to the floor. Percy dropped to help her, catching a glimpse of a limp, cold body that was definitely *not* Mark Richmond.

The doctor rushed to tend to Ellen.

"It's not him," gasped Percy, fanning the unconscious Ellen.

"Are you sure?"

"I was just with the Richmonds a few days ago, and I can categorically state that the man lying on the slab is not him. Mark has all his hair, is a lot slimmer than the chap on the table, and much taller. Plus, Mark does not have a mole on his forehead."

"Then who in the world is he?" demanded the coroner.

"I don't recognize him," she said, "but Mrs. Richmond may when she wakes up."

"Do you have any idea why he might have had Mr. Richmond's identification?"

Percy did not feel she had the authority to spill the beans on Mark Richmond's nefarious business dealings and shook her head. The doctor placed a pillow under Ellen and dangled some smelling salts under her nose. Her fearful eyes opened, swinging between Percy and the doctor.

"Do you remember what happened?" Percy asked her.

Biting her lip, Ellen nodded. "It's not Mark," she whispered. "But the stress of worry overcame me, and I passed out."

"Do you know who it is? Do you recognize him?" Percy continued.

"I've never seen him before," she murmured.

Between them, the coroner and Percy helped Ellen to her feet, guiding her to a little room with some chairs and a table. The medical examiner disappeared then returned bringing Ellen some tea.

"I need to get back to work," he explained.

"Of course," said Percy. "We'll be fine now."

As soon as he was gone, Ellen said, "Then where is my husband?"

"Could he be in hiding? If loan sharks are after him, he may have needed to lay low while he tried to raise some funds."

"Then why hasn't he contacted me?" Ellen cried, eyes frantic.

"To keep you out of danger?" suggested Percy.

"Danger?" She grabbed Percy by the collar, making her choke. "The children are alone. I need to get back!" She staggered for the door, smashing her bag against her chest.

Percy reached for her arm. "Take a moment to think. You are simply reacting. How can you best protect your family?"

Ellen's jaw tanked. "Mother."

"I think that's probably the best solution. They may come looking for Mark at your house. As the pair of you already discussed, doing a disappearing act of your own may be the wisest thing to do."

"If he's not already dead," said Ellen through her tears. "I'll kill him when he resurfaces."

Percy hoped it was merely a turn of phrase.

Chapter 17

Percy arrived home well before a scrumptious dinner of fish pie and mashed potato and was now cuddled up to both boys by a roaring fire, listening to a serialized story that Bartie had requested. Before they turned off the wireless, they listened to the shipping forecast. It was strangely calming after a terrifying and chaotic day.

"Can we go to a bookstore tomorrow?" Bartie asked. "I think we should buy Daddy a new history book for Christmas."

"That's a splendid idea," she responded. "And how about I make it a special outing to make up for being gone so much by driving you to *Blackburn's?*" It was one of the biggest bookstores in the country and specialized in hard-to-find books—a bookworm's paradise.

"Really?" shouted Bartie. "Wahoo!" And he and William did a little jig around the room, filling Percy with love for her little men.

After a hearty breakfast, they bundled into the car and set out on their adventure. The boys were so excited they couldn't stop singing or whistling. The famous bookstore was in a pretty town anchored by a steepled church set in a shallow valley. Along the gaily decorated high street were many Elizabethan buildings with their soot black beams and whitewashed walls, housing upscale dress shops, chemists, and the popular bookstore.

The street had been forged long before motor vehicles were invented and was far too narrow for the modern methods of travel. It was bursting with Christmas shoppers, cars, bicycles and trams and just as Percy had spotted a vacant parking spot, a large Rolls Royce slipped into it.

"Bother!"

She pulled away and drove around the block to try her luck again. This time a small car was indicating that it was leaving, farther from the store, but she stopped to wait, in case a closer one did not open up. Though the way was clear, the driver seemed reluctant to pull out into traffic. Percy waved her arm to assure the timid driver that the road was open and as she did so, was startled to see Phoebe Valentine leaving the bookstore. Too far away to call out to her, she watched as Phoebe bounced along the pavement, wondering what her friend was doing so far from home.

The nervous driver still delayed, and Percy felt her hackles rise. She looked behind her to see a stream of cars waiting and waved encouragement to the unsure driver again. This time, the car poked its nose ever so slightly into the street but then jerked to a stop. Irritated, Percy flung her arms in the air and as she did so, spotted a man who looked very much like Bruce Goodfellow, enter the bookstore.

How strange!

But Jemima *had* mentioned that he had developed a recent habit of reading.

Bringing her back to the tricky situation at hand, a cacophony of horns sounded as the drivers behind her became impatient.

However, rather than pull out, the hesitant, young woman driver hopped out of the vehicle and onto the pavement, flapping her arms in distress. Thankfully, a passing pedestrian stopped to aid her. She pointed at her car, then the man slipped into the stranded vehicle and pulled out into the street, waiting for the young woman to replace him. This time the chorus of horns were sounded in celebration.

Finally.

Percy nosed her car into the spot just as Bruce exited the store holding a book. He hurried across the street where he jumped into a waiting taxi which sped off in the opposite direction.

106

Curious.

As the bell above the door rang, Percy's nose filled with book leather, paper, dust, and lavender. The boys ran in ahead of her, straight to the children's section. Percy made for the checkout desk.

"I'm looking for books on British history," she began as the tiny cashier stuck another pencil through her graying bun.

"Medieval, or Victorian?" Mouselike eyes and nose twitched as she waited for Percy's response, reminding her of the dream.

"Victorian, I think."

Was her choice affected by the bookshop keeper's dress? She couldn't say but followed her as she scurried to a stack of books near the back of the burrowlike interior. The middle-aged lady stopped abruptly, and Percy had to hold onto a shelf in order to avoid a collision.

The mousy woman gestured to the whole aisle. "I think you will find what you are looking for."

As she made to leave, Percy blocked the aisle. "I thought I saw a friend of mine, a couple of them actually, leaving as I was arriving. I'm wondering if she is a regular customer."

The woman tipped her head and wrinkled her nose. If she had sprouted whiskers Percy would not have been surprised.

"Her name is Phoebe Valentine," added Percy.

The mouse shook her head as though she were flicking water from her hair. "No one by that name. I know most of my regulars."

"Do you work here often?" Percy asked.

The woman pulled herself to full height which was still only to Percy's chest.

"*I* am the owner of this bookstore," she said regally.

"A thousand apologies," cowered Percy. "Well, you must know everyone who comes in. The woman I'm

107

speaking of is about my age but much prettier. Blonde hair, bright blue eyes. Very graceful manners. She left not ten minutes ago."

The shopkeeper's eyes narrowed. "That sounds like Miranda Cusworth."

Miranda? Why would Phoebe need to use a false name?

"And the other person is Bruce Goodfellow," Percy continued.

The mouse's face went blank.

"Exceptionally handsome, tall, dark. He left about five minutes ago."

"Oh! I think you mean Arthur Millbrook. He's a regular customer. Very chivalrous man. Buys a book at least twice a month. Lovely person."

"My mistake." But Percy knew she was not mistaken.

They had left the bookstore with four books, one for each of the boys, one for Piers for Christmas, and a leatherbound collection of sonnets for her mother who only admired highbrow gifts. All the way home, Percy had puzzled about her friends' use of pseudonyms.

"Another affair?" suggested Mrs. Appleby as they ate dessert after dinner that night.

Percy's shoulders sank. "Are all my friends' lives falling apart?"

"What other reason would they have for using false names and meeting in out of the way places?" Mrs. Appleby emphasized.

"But they weren't in the bookstore *together*. Phoebe left before Bruce arrived."

"All I know is, it's suspicious," said the cook.

After dinner and a game of Monopoly by the fire, Percy went up to William's room. Winning the game had put Bartie in a decent mood, and he wandered in holding the adventure book he had purchased that day.

108

"Can you read this to us?" he asked.

Percy's heart skipped. "Of course."

The three of them snuggled into William's bed and Percy basked in the warm presence of both her children.

"*The Crippled Spy* by John Ashworth." She cleared her throat preparing to do all the voices.

The story began with a gripping scene and both boys were riveted. The main character was injured at the beginning of the Great War and sent home. Desperate to continue to help in the war effort, in spite of a limp, he enlisted as a spy.

By the third chapter, William was gently snoring, still leaning against her arm.

"Shall I go on?" she asked Bartie.

"Let's do one more chapter."

The main character recruited the help of a woman, a woman from a different walk of life. To avoid being seen together, they passed messages to each other through books at the library.

Percy dropped the story to her lap. "That's it!" she cried.

"What?" asked Bartie, confused.

Percy retrieved the book from the bedspread. "Oh, nothing. Sorry. Just something I've been puzzling about all evening."

She read the rest of the chapter but would not have remembered one thing about it if asked. After kissing Bartie on the head and tucking him into his own bed, she ran downstairs, where Mrs. Appleby was making Horlicks.

"I know what they're doing!" Percy cried as she crashed through the kitchen door.

Mrs. Appleby, hand to chest, gasped. "Who?"

"Phoebe and Bruce. I think they're spies."

"What on earth led to that conclusion?" the cook asked. "Doesn't she have three young children?"

Percy explained about the book she had just read. "Instead of a library they're using the bookstore. Phoebe must place a message in a pre-arranged book and Bruce goes in and buys it right after."

Rather than celebrating her brilliance, Mrs. Appleby put a hand over one eye. "It's a bit of a stretch."

"But it would explain so many things," Percy protested. "The use of false names, not being in the store at the same time, choosing somewhere far from their homes. What else would explain all that?"

The cook flattened her lips and considered. "An affair would explain them. Rather than spies, perhaps they leave messages about illicit assignations."

Eyes wide, Percy exclaimed. "I think you've been watching too many films, Mrs. Appleby." The cook had every Wednesday afternoon off and would often spend it at the local cinema.

"It's a lot less far-fetched than your suggestion, if you don't mind me saying so," contested the cook.

Percy folded her arms. "You were the one who suggested I try sleuthing for a hobby. I need more proof. I shall have to follow Phoebe."

"You don't know her movements," said Mrs. Appleby as she dried the dishes and put them away.

"I shall call and ask to come to tea again and if she can't make it I will know she has an appointment...or assignation," declared Percy.

Percy, wearing a black scarf pulled tightly over her frizzy locks, was currently waiting for Phoebe to come out of *Thornbury's* department store. It was rather difficult for a six-foot woman to melt into a crowd, but she was sitting at a Lyon's tea house across the street and looking through the window.

Her next visit for tea with Phoebe was two days from now but while trying to schedule it, Phoebe had mentioned she was busy for the next two days. Percy had installed herself behind a tree at the bottom of the lane that led to Phoebe's house. After two wasted hours, Phoebe's dark blue car finally pulled into the t-junction and turned toward the town. Percy followed at a comfortable distance, a spark in her veins. Sleuthing was rather fun.

When Phoebe went into the department store, Percy decided to watch from afar in case she ran into her friend. After three cups of tea and two cakes, Percy was desperate for the loo but, worried that Phoebe would leave while she was gone, she held it.

Thirty minutes later, Phoebe appeared with two hat boxes and three garment bags. She threw them into the back of her car and headed off. Percy's brain was screaming at her to use the facilities, but she ignored it and ran for her car.

A fine winter rain was now falling, and her windscreen wipers were having trouble keeping up with the task. She peered through the smeared glass trying to keep an eye on Phoebe's car which was headed out of the town. It was soon evident that Phoebe was driving in the direction of her home and deflated, Percy sailed past the turning for Phoebe's house, headed toward her own home.

A shopping trip! What a bally waste of time.

Perhaps sleuthing wasn't so fun.

Chapter 18

After Mrs. Appleby had stopped laughing about Percy's escapades, after dinner, Percy dug deep in her junk drawer for a dog-eared notebook and a chewed pencil. It was time to get things straight.

The inspector had called while she was out to make an appointment to see her in two days and she wanted to get everything she had learned out of her head and onto paper for the interview. She wrote the names of her friends in a list.

"Now, what is the first thing a detective looks for?" she asked Mrs. Appleby.

"Well, you need the *who*, the *how* and the *why*," replied her cook as she took the dessert she was baking out of the Aga. "Least that's what the detectives in the novels say."

"Perhaps I should start reading some." Percy sucked the end of the pencil. "We know the *how*. It was a rolling pin and anyone could have used it. I'm going to guess there were no usable fingerprints on it or there might have been an arrest already. Now, what about the who?" She dragged the end of the soggy pencil down her list.

"Ellen says she and Mark were up late discussing their troubles. She heard a giggle. Men don't giggle so it must have been a woman and she sounded like she was flirting. That leaves Jemima, Verity and Phoebe."

"And a woman wouldn't giggle alone," said Mrs. Appleby, cutting a large slice of the Bakewell tart and sliding it across the table to Percy. She thought about refusing it—she'd had trouble zipping up her skirt that morning—but chewing helped her think, so eating it was in the pursuit of justice.

"And why would two women be up after two in the morning giggling? So, I think it's safe to say the woman was probably with a man."

Mrs. Appleby pointed her fork at Percy. "Didn't you say Mrs. Howard was messing around with the gardener? Could it have been him?"

"I admit I thought the same thing," Percy said. "I need to find out if the gardener has an alibi."

"And how do you propose to do that?"

Percy thought for a minute. "I shall call Tom for a reference. Tell him I'm looking for a new gardener and ask if he would recommend his."

"It's a bit far from here," said Mrs. Appleby, pouring some more double cream on the tart. Percy eyed it with envy and after deliberating for half a minute grabbed the jug herself and drowned her own piece.

"He's a man, he probably won't even think about that or he'll think I'm a dunce which he probably thinks anyway. That's job number one." She wrote, *Call Tom*.

"What about the other women?"

"Phoebe has to be on the list because of the strange behavior of frequenting the same bookstore as Bruce and using a pseudonym." She underlined Phoebe's name. "And she lost a red crystal from a necklace in the kitchen. I found it the next day when I was having another snack. Then I forgot all about it and Phoebe didn't mention it. Actually, she had lost a valuable pearl earring and we were all searching the house for it. But I know she was wearing the red necklace at the party and that she was not wearing it the following day. The next time I saw it, the piece was on the neck of her young daughter."

"She could have gone into the kitchen at any time before the murder and lost it," pointed out the cook.

"I don't think so. I noticed the pretty necklace at dinner and then we were all together until we went up to bed. She would have had to enter the kitchen *after* midnight."

"That's two strikes against *her*, then," said Mrs. Appleby putting on the kettle.

113

"And she is busy tomorrow afternoon. I'm going to take a chance and go back to the bookstore and hide in the stacks."

"You? Hide?" Mrs. Appleby chuckled.

"I know. I'm not easily invisible but I've thought about it and I'm going to wear a disguise. I'll dress as a man by borrowing some of Pier's brown and beige clothes and I'll blend right into the books and shelves."

"That should be good for a laugh," said the cook, wiping her eye.

"Ok, back to the midnight giggle."

"I thought you said it was after two o'clock in the morning?" said Mrs. Appleby.

"It was, but that doesn't flow as well as the word 'midnight'." She looked at her list. "That leaves Jemima. Honestly, I don't think she has the backbone for murder."

"But what about hanky panky?" Mrs. Appleby was enjoying this far too much.

"You've met her. Do you really think Tom or Walter would pursue her?" Percy thought of the timid woman with the extra pounds, the style of a nun and the personality of a brick.

"It's always the least obvious person in the whodunnits," Mrs. Appleby reminded her.

"Well, this is real life. Though I cannot cast her as the lover, she *did* say she was worried about Bruce. And the meeting at the bookstore seems to validate her fears about him."

"What if Bruce met Phoebe in the kitchen for a clandestine meeting and Jemima caught them?"

Percy considered the suggestion for a minute. "Then why would Jemima hit the cook?"

Mrs. Appleby pursed her lips. "It was dark and maybe she thought she was hitting Phoebe?"

A rumble of laughter tickled Percy's tummy and traveled up and out of her mouth. "That might have been a

114

bit awkward the next morning. Three of them would have known who the killer was. I don't think that's plausible."

"Well, when you put it like that…" The cook cupped her chin with her hand.

Percy had a flash of intelligence. "I doubt the killer would have been giggling in the hallway after the murder. They would have hightailed it back to their rooms so as not to be caught. I think they are two different events."

"Good point! Did anyone say their spouse was gone for a bit?"

"We were pretty plastered when we went to bed. I would think most people crashed right out. I know I did. It was my bladder that woke me up." She slapped the table. "That reminds me, Jemima said Bruce did go to the loo."

"That's when I miss my chamber pot," said Mrs. Appleby. "It was much more convenient to pull out the china pot, do your business and push it back under. No need to go wandering around in the dark."

Percy was not sure she agreed. Crouching her six feet to the floor was a lot of trouble and she, for one, was glad to trade it for a trip to the lavatory. She wrote 'toilet' next to Bruce's name.

"I think I'm going to cross Ellen and Mark off," she said. "They were discussing their troubles well into the early morning."

"What if the lender came to confront them in the house and bumped into the cook in the kitchen? He'd have no problem bumping her off."

Mrs. Appleby was surprising Percy with her active imagination. "I think the police would have noticed large footprints coming into the house, don't you? Oh! I suppose that rules the gardener out too. His footprints only went to the shed. Unless he hid somewhere in the house until the wee hours." She ran a light line through the Richmond's names.

"You're doing very well, Mrs. Pontefract. You have a knack for mystery."

"I am, aren't I? And except for surveillance, it's rather fun." She mentally apologized to Mrs. Barlow for finding her murder *fun*. "I also need to consider the men. Whopping someone on the head is more of a male thing. It would take a lot of umph."

She looked at the list and crossed off Walter. He would not have been able to make it up the stairs fast enough with his artificial leg. "I don't believe Walter could have climbed the stairs in time, but perhaps I could ask him if Phoebe was in their room all night. He was drinking very heavily the whole time we were there, so he may have slept soundly, but it wouldn't hurt to ask." One thing she was not good at was subtlety. She would have to plan out how to ask him without being obvious.

That left Bruce and Tom.

Bruce's other activities were questionable, which was a strike against him and she made a note to ask Verity if Tom had been in bed up until the screaming alerted everyone.

She snapped her fingers. "What if Tom suspected Verity and the gardener, and was waiting to catch them in a compromising situation in the kitchen and mistook the cook for the gardener?"

"If Mr. Howard had killed Mrs. Barlow by mistake, wouldn't he have told the police that it was a terrible accident and he thought she was an intruder?"

"Oh, yes. Bother!" She put down the pencil. "My brain hurts. I think it's time to go and read to the boys. I'll get to my 'to do' list tomorrow."

"Hello, Tom? Yes, it's Percy. Look, I'll get straight to the point. I am in the market for a new gardener, and I wondered if you would recommend yours."

"It's a bit far from you, isn't it?" he responded.

Drat! "I thought perhaps he might have friends in the business that he could recommend that are closer to me." Did that sound credible? She was no good at lying under pressure. "I just need his number."

A huff and some rustling sounds ensued and then Tom came back on the line. "Ready?"

"Yes."

"Billy Brogan. Hampstead 455. That's the main house line. He's a lodger there. He doesn't have his own telephone."

She scribbled it down. "Thanks ever so."

They said goodbye and she dialed the number he had given her.

"Hampstead 455." The accent was from Yorkshire.

Percy put on her best voice. "Hello, I am trying to contact Mr. Brogan."

"He's not here right now but I can take a message."

Percy left her number and the reason for her call then decided to pump the woman for information.

"I met Mr. Brogan at the Howard's. I was very impressed with the way he had pruned their roses." She dropped the bait. "It was the day after the terrible murder."

"I read about that in the paper and I said to Mr. Brogan, 'You better choose your clients more carefully. Those fancy people 'aving a murder at their house.' And then the police called us and wanted to talk to 'im about 'is whereabouts and I said it was lucky my plumbing went out that night because he 'elped me with my flooded kitchen until three in the morning and I could tell the copper 'e was 'ere with me."

Hmmm. Percy chewed her lip and crossed out Billy Brogan's name.

"That *was* fortunate for him. Well, if you'll let him know I called. Thank you."

She would just have Mrs. Appleby answer the phone and take a message and then let the contact die on the vine.

117

She looked down at her list.

Should she tell Jemima about seeing Bruce at the bookstore?

Chapter 19

The Pontefracts had the paper delivered every morning for Piers. These days he seemed to be gone more than he was there, and Percy had developed the habit of reading the paper with her breakfast. She shuffled her way into the warm and friendly kitchen. Mrs. Appleby placed a bowl of steaming oats and honey in front of her. The boys were not up yet. She shook out the paper and dropped it almost at once. There on the front page was a picture of Walter, looking stunned. The headline screamed,

High Profile Surgeon Struck off Register as Charges Brought by Dead Patient's Family!

Percy's mind reviewed the article she had seen at the Howard's. *The unnamed doctor was Walter!*

She ran her finger along the article.

Walter Valentine, respected surgeon, is accused of malpractice by the family of a patient they claim died on the table under the hands of the doctor. They accuse him of arriving in the theater drunk. Since the suit has been publicized, several other patients have come forward with similar claims.

Percy thought of the many times she had seen Walter drinking from a tumbler of whiskey at the Howard's, and his unexpected arrival at home the day she and the children visited. Something had passed between the spouses when he burst into the living room and seeing this article made Percy think that he had been furloughed pending the outcome of the trial.

Could the Howard's cook have had some connection to the dead patient? Did she, perhaps, try to blackmail Walter? Percy tried to imagine the injured Walter speeding up the stairs after killing the cook. It just wasn't possible. Did Phoebe commit the crime on behalf of her husband? She needed to get back over to the Valentines. There were so many unanswered questions.

But first, she was going back to *Blackburns* for more surveillance.

Avoiding the bookstore owner, Percy had settled herself in a far corner of the store that had a clear view of the door. Dressed in brown, wool slacks and a beige, corduroy jacket with one of Pier's caps pulled down over her eyes, she had timed her visit for an hour before she had come before.

Her legs were starting to ache, and she was wishing she had popped a snack in her pocket, when the bell above the door rang for the hundredth time since she had arrived. She was beginning to wonder if she should open her own book shop. She glanced up from the World Atlas she was holding and jerked.

It was Phoebe.

Percy pulled her cap farther down and sidled to the front of her stack, peering around the end. She was in time to see Phoebe pull a book from the shelf, open it, place a paper inside and reshelve it. Her heart started hammering. Phoebe glanced up and Percy turned her head just in time. She waited a minute before checking again but Phoebe was already making for the register.

She bought a small book, chatting with the rodent-like shopkeeper then bounced out of the store.

Deciding she had, at most, five minutes, Percy hurried to the stack where Phoebe had planted the paper. Fortunately, the book had not been pushed in all the way and Percy grabbed it with trembling hands, flicking through the pages. Someone entered the stack and she nearly fainted, but it was a boy of about fifteen. She clasped the book to her chest as he went by. Once he was gone, she looked at the paper. It was a series of numbers and meant absolutely nothing to Percy. She replaced the paper and closed the book, careful to reshelve it just as she had found it and hurried back to her atlas. As she opened the large edition, the bell rang again and Bruce entered. Heart in her mouth, Percy turned her back to him, hunched over the book, then walked backward to the end of her row. Turning her head to the left, she watched as he removed the book she had just handled and headed to the register. He carried on a pleasant conversation with the little owner, complimenting her on her hair and the orderliness of the store and then hurried out the door. Percy watched as he again jumped into a taxi.

All the other theories she had come up with faded away. She was sure this was why the cook had been killed, but for the life of her she couldn't see how.

Chapter 20

Ripping off the masculine hat, Percy put the car in gear and swung out of her parking space. Gripping the steering wheel so tightly her fingers went numb, she pressed the accelerator to the floor, wishing that her little Ford could travel faster than thirty miles an hour. As she hurtled through the English countryside, her mind raging with jumbled facts about the people at the fated Christmas party, she knew she had to call the inspector and tell him what she had discovered and her theory. But until she could organize it in writing it was merely a morass of disconnected items.

Kicking up gravel in the driveway, the car screeched to a stop, she flung open the door and raced inside. Mrs. Appleby's smile vanished when she saw her mistress.

"Where are the boys?" Percy demanded.

"Outside playing soldiers. You look like you need a cup of tea. What happened?"

"I hardly know but Bruce and Phoebe are not innocent."

"Of the murder?"

"I think so. Uggh!" Her hands were ransacking the kitchen drawer. "Where is my notebook?"

Looking fearful, Mrs. Appleby pulled the pad from beside the Aga. "I put it somewhere for safekeeping. Here."

Percy grabbed it. "I'm sorry to worry you but my mind is in shambles and I need to write everything down and call the police."

Mrs. Appleby dropped into the chair across the table. "You look awful."

"I feel awful," she agreed. "When your friends are theoretical murderers, it is one thing, but when you uncover possible evidence that they actually *did* commit the crime, it changes everything. I feel quite sick."

Mrs. Appleby thrust the sweet tea at her and she took a large gulp.

"Tell me everything and then you can get it written down," suggested the cook.

Percy relayed everything that happened in the famous bookstore. Mrs. Appleby frowned. "Certainly suspicious but how does this connect to the cook's murder?"

"I'm still missing a piece, but those numbers I found in the book have to be significant. It could be a code or coordinates. And the fact that Phoebe and Bruce were already in some kind of partnership for this nefarious scheme before the Howard's party, must account for something." She had a sudden recollection that Ellen had said Phoebe was pale as a ghost looking over the stairs when Tom ran down to see what Percy was screaming about.

"Phoebe and Bruce have some kind of classified information swap going on, else why the need for secrecy?" she said, pushing her pencil so hard into the paper that the lead snapped. Mrs. Appleby jumped up, rummaged in the drawer and handed her another pencil.

Percy took a calming breath. "Some of this will be guesswork but I can have the inspector follow up on it for the facts.

"Bruce and Phoebe must have needed to talk in person that night about something classified. I remember finding a scrap of paper with the partial words 'eet 2' on it. I would wager that the full note said, *Let's meet. At 2 in kitchen.*" Percy startled Mrs. Appleby by jumping up and rushing into the hall to find her handbag, praying she had kept the sliver of paper. Her fingers hit the crystal and she pulled it out. Glinting in the light from the window, Percy knew it must be further damning evidence. She popped it in her pocket and foraged some more before finally landing on the little fragment. She kissed it and ran back to the kitchen, laying the crystal and snippet on the table.

"Now, I don't know exactly what their meeting was about, but for some reason, Mrs. Barlow went to the kitchen in the middle of the night. Perhaps like me, she had gone to the lavatory and then felt peckish and thought about the leftover food. If Bruce and Phoebe were meeting in the kitchen, Mrs. Barlow would have heard noises in the pantry and opened the door. In the shock of the moment, Bruce would have grabbed whatever was to hand to extinguish the perceived threat. They could not know whether she had overheard them talking about sensitive things or not. If they *are* spies, it could have been matters of national security which would be considered treasonous."

Mrs. Appleby's hands flew to her mouth. "You think they're traitors?"

At that very moment, William and Bartie fell through the back door into the mudroom, laughing and crashing.

Percy locked eyes with Mrs. Appleby.

"Mum! You're back!" shouted William, sliding into the kitchen on stockinged feet. He frowned. "Why are you wearing Daddy's clothes?"

She looked down at her legs, her mind stuttering.

"I'm going to take up the hem for your father," said Mrs. Appleby. "I thought it would be easier to do if someone was wearing them."

Behind the boys' heads, Percy's face scrunched up, but the boys accepted the lie at face value.

"Last one up the stairs is a lemon!" cried Bartie, flying for the door.

"Well done, Mrs. A!" said Percy. "Now, where was I?"

"Treason," said the cook somberly.

"Oh, yes." She picked up the pencil. "They would have fled the scene as quickly as possible. Perhaps they heard the Richmond's talking when they got up the stairs and worried that someone was up, pretended that they were a romantic couple meeting in the dark—hence the flirty giggle. That seems better than any other explanation I can come up with."

"So now we know the how and the who. But what would drive them to commit treason?" asked the cook.

Percy leaned back in her chair. "Think! Think!" She pounded the table with a fist. "Money!"

"You'll have to explain it to me," said Mrs. Appleby.

"Walter was already in trouble. I read about it in the paper. I think he's an alcoholic and it was affecting his work. A patient died which began a probe. According to the article, it is not going to end well for him. He and Phoebe must have known he was likely to lose his license and thus their source of income.

"Phoebe's father works for the government. I believe he's involved in top secret stuff at the Ministry of Defence. I imagine she thought she could make money from selling his secrets. Reading files, listening at doors, etc… I don't know how Phoebe and Bruce became partners in crime, perhaps Phoebe mentioned their financial worries and Bruce recruited her, but I've seen the Valentine's new house. It must have cost a fortune, and it takes a small army of servants to run. I bet the story about the uncle dying and leaving all his money to Bruce is a lie." She thought of the expensive diamond cufflinks and sighing, rested her head in her hands. "At least they didn't commit pre-meditated murder."

"But if they're found guilty of treason, they will hang," said Mrs. Appleby. "Those poor children."

Percy's head was banging and all she wanted to do was lay down or take a bath, but she had a job to do. She dragged herself up the stairs, took off her husband's clothes to change into a more appropriate outfit, and went to call the inspector.

After greeting her with a surly attitude, the inspector was unusually quiet as Percy detailed her experience at the bookstore. He remained quiet as she explained about the items she had discovered during the search for the missing earring and when the chair had squealed on the kitchen floor. Items that now seemed to be smoking guns.

As she spoke, a memory was jogged loose. She reviewed how surprised she had been when Phoebe had come back from the direction of the kitchen when she was supposed to be looking for the pearl earring in her room. Was the whole thing a ruse to give her time to search for the red crystal? She told the inspector of her recollection.

"If you post a plain clothes man at the bookstore, you will catch them at their game, Inspector. Then when you bring them in for questioning, you can present the portion of the note and the red crystal. With a good lawyer they may get off the charge of murder, but if they *are* selling government secrets, no one will be able to save them from the noose."

"Well, I admire your grit, Mrs. Pontefract," said the inspector, the crotchety attitude replaced by a measure of admiration. "It could not have been easy to tell me all this about your friends. Of course, there are still a lot of questions that need answering and a great deal of good, old fashioned police work to undertake, but I don't mind telling you that my investigation had stalled. These are valuable leads and I thank you."

"That is extremely gracious of you, Inspector. It appears that Mrs. Barlow was just in the wrong place at the wrong time. What a waste of a life," she said.

"You do realize that, but for a few minutes, it could have been *you* who was bashed on the head."

The thought made Percy's stomach roll.

"How do you do it, Inspector?"

"I'm not sure I understand your meaning, Mrs. Pontefract?"

"Day in, day out witnessing human behavior at its worst. It is so depressing."

"Justice is what keeps me going," he declared. "Finding the murderer; settling the score."

126

"I'm grateful there are men such as yourself who dedicate themselves to this work. I'm not sure I ever want to do anything like this again."

Chapter 21

Percy woke with a jolt. She was supposed to have tea with Phoebe today! *Crikey!* How would she ever act naturally after she had divulged everything to the inspector? The police did not have enough evidence to arrest Phoebe yet, but she knew they were busy gathering it. The inspector had suggested she keep her appointment so as not to alert Phoebe that anything was wrong. Percy sat up feeling as though she had swallowed a hive of bees.

She skipped breakfast.

The boys awoke with oodles of energy. Percy suggested they all go for a walk. They spent the morning roaming the frosty woods with their energetic dog, Percy withdrawn into her worries. The children were running ahead, shrieking, and throwing sticks for Apollo. They didn't seem to notice her sullen mood. The temperature had pushed its nose over freezing point causing the snow to melt and transforming hard pathways into gooey mud that crept over her green, rubber boots.

Pondering whether she should cancel her afternoon plans in spite of what the inspector said, she reluctantly packed the boys into the car after lunch. They sang rousing carols as she drove which helped keep her mind off the daunting task ahead. She must not let her behavior betray that she knew anything.

As she pulled into the Valentine's driveway, she let the car idle at the top of the lane.

"Mum, what are you waiting for?" asked William who was eager to start playing with Phoebe's daughter.

"I was just thinking how pretty their house is," she fudged, inching her way down the driveway.

Phoebe answered the door with the barking dogs, and the adorable toddler gripping her leg with one hand, the thumb of the other stuck in his mouth. Percy felt her resolve fade. *Why had she come?* The knowledge she possessed was weighing on her mind and she thought about the consequences for this trusting little person.

The boys disappeared with their friends as soon as they entered the welcoming foyer, and she and Phoebe went into the comfortable, snug sitting room. Since she had last been there, the family had set up their tree in the corner of the room. *Normal. Traditional. Safe.* The wheels Percy has set in motion where about to rip it all apart.

Phoebe caught Percy looking at the tree. "It's from the bottom of the garden. Isn't it perfect?"

Percy was amazed that Phoebe could act naturally. Had she grown so hardened to her crimes that a murder did not affect her? Percy's conscience would be crippling her at this point.

They labored through a stilted conversation as the tiny boy demanded his mother's attention and Percy couldn't help watching the clock.

Her nose began to tickle, and she dug through her handbag in search of a clean handkerchief but the sneeze attacked her before she was ready, erupting like an explosion of Vesuvius and causing her hand to fling the handkerchief out of the bag. A little projectile flew out with it, landing on the small table by the settee.

When Percy had recovered, Phoebe was staring at a small, red crystal.

Percy gulped as Phoebe raised terrified eyes.

"Where did that come from?" she asked in a tiny voice.

"The Howard's kitchen." The words were few but laden with meaning.

Phoebe's lip began to tremble, and she hugged the boy to her like a shield, peering into Percy's eyes as if trying to read her mind.

"I wondered where it had gone."

Percy didn't know whether to stay quiet or tell Phoebe what she had done. It was a watershed moment, and

129

everything was riding on it. Would Phoebe turn violent as she had that night in the Howard's kitchen? Percy had to be careful—her children were in the house.

The ticking of an ancient clock was the only sound and Percy's heart was in her throat.

"It wasn't me," Phoebe finally said.

Percy considered playing dumb, but it was obvious Phoebe understood her predicament.

"It was Bruce." A naked confession.

Percy wanted to flee, to race up the stairs, drag the boys out and punch the accelerator on the car but she suddenly realized that the children were the buffer. The very thing that would prevent Phoebe becoming violent. The toddler's head was resting on his mother's shoulder, eyes closed, thumb firmly stuck. Still, Percy could not find words.

"Bruce and I were meeting in the pantry about…some business. Important business. Delicate. When the door was yanked open revealing the cook we were bewildered, and Bruce panicked. He picked up the closest thing and struck. I was horrified. Horrified!

"We ran back to our rooms, with a feeling of doom. The actions of a split second were going to destroy our lives." Tears trickled over Phoebe's lids and slid down her perfect cheeks.

"But the police came, and we were not arrested. I was so relieved. It seemed as though we were going to get away with it and I relaxed." She flashed shiny eyes to Percy. "I felt horrid about it, you understand. Terrible. A human life had been lost. That's why I went to the funeral. Mrs. Barlow was just in the wrong place at the wrong time. It was tragic."

Percy's own words coming out of the mouth of a murderer made her shiver.

"What are you going to do?" Phoebe asked after a few minutes.

"It's already done."

130

The beautiful, shining eyes flared. "Done?"

"I was at *Blackburn's*."

"Oh." There was so much meaning in that short expression.

Percy took a deep breath. "I know you all think I'm a bit of a social disaster, but it turns out I have a knack for deduction. I put the pieces together and created a theory. I tested my hypothesis and witnessed for myself the exchange of information."

Phoebe's eyes and forehead creased with confusion.

"The tall man with the atlas in the bookstore? That was me."

Nodding, Phoebe's skin smoothed.

"I told the inspector everything," Percy resumed. "They're surveilling the bookstore as we speak."

Phoebe's head dropped, and her shoulders began to shake.

"Why? Why did you do it?" asked Percy.

"Alcoholism is the very devil!" whined Phoebe. "It has become Walter's mistress. When he told me what had happened during the surgery, I knew we were going to lose everything and I was not going to let that happen.

"Walter has never recovered from the war. As a doctor he saw such atrocities. He couldn't get them out of his head, but if he drank, the pain lessened. And losing his leg. He has mourned that every bit as much as losing a parent or a friend. He was out in the field, performing triage, making sure those who were alive but severely injured were given priority, when he stepped on a landmine. It is painful to stand for surgery. I think the alcohol reduced the physical pain too." She wiped her cheek. "It seemed like providence when I was walking by Daddy's home office one day, and I heard him in deep conversation with someone. I knew he was an important figure in the Ministry of Defence but he never talked about his work. Hearing him, I was curious, and listened at the door. The things I heard that day were the stuff of Hollywood films.

"Not long after that, I met up with Jemima. I was having a bad day and told her some of my troubles. She must have mentioned it to Bruce because he showed up when I was shopping, a few days later, and recruited me. The kind of money he was offering would make all my worries disappear, and I convinced myself if I was just sharing secrets, no one would get hurt." A sob escaped and the baby stirred. "I was wrong."

The guilt-free manner was swept away in an instant, like a broom cutting through spider's webs, replaced by fear and alarm. Percy searched Phoebe's face for shades of remorse at causing the death of an innocent person. She saw none. The regret etched in Phoebe's features was all for her children. The bitter heartbreak, as Phoebe realized what her children would suffer, would haunt Percy for a long time to come.

Chapter 22

"Darling!" *Piers.*

The police had come to take Phoebe into custody after her confession. It had all been very low key so as not to upset the children. Bruce's arrest, on the other hand, had been sensational, cameras flashing as he was hauled away in handcuffs. Inspector Brown had set up a fake information swap at the bookstore and caught him red-handed. The emotional toll of everything had left Percy drained. Her legs and lips wobbled at the sound of her husband's voice, and she plonked her exhausted body in a chair as she gripped the earpiece.

"Hello, Piers."

"I just saw the headlines," he said. "I can't believe it! Bruce has been my friend through thick and thin. I'm so sorry I haven't been able to be with you. Was it awful?"

She reflected back on the last couple of weeks. It was not *all* awful. The boys had been her pole star in a difficult time, but everything else had been pretty atrocious. Should she tell him it was she who found the body? It had not been made public, at her request. *No, not on the telephone.* That was the stuff of pillow talk, intimate, private.

"Let's just say I think that will be the last ever annual Howard Christmas Party, and I will not be sorry about it."

She heard his somber chuckle through the line. "Percy, you always were able to find humor in the darkest of moments. It's just one of the things I love about you."

Her heart skipped. Piers was not one for romantic language, as a rule, which made each tender endearment that much more significant.

"Thank you."

"I'm still reeling from the fact that dainty Phoebe Valentine was selling government secrets," he continued. "Boggles the mind."

"Walter was going to lose his license to practice medicine because of his drinking problem. It seemed like a way out of financial ruin when Bruce suggested it."

"I can't imagine being so desperate I would betray my country," he blustered. "And Bruce, well, there's just no excuse."

She pushed wild curls behind her ear. "He had become accustomed to the finer things of life and his government salary would not cover it," she explained.

"They deserve their punishment." Piers was not a harsh man, but he was a fiercely patriotic one. She imagined in *his* mind, the crime of treason was worse than infidelity. "But it is hard to think that my childhood friend group has been shattered," he opined.

"The court date is set for the beginning of January," Percy added. "So, it will be a rotten Christmas for their families."

"Well, they should have thought of that before." His indignation was growing.

"I shall be called as a witness," she admitted. "I think the whole house party will be called." He didn't need to know why just yet.

"Really? I shall try to come with you."

The large, yawning pit that had taken up residence in her stomach since the arrests, closed just a little. "I'd like that."

"Look, I know I've been gone a lot and missed some fun with the boys, but I talked to my boss and he's going to let me come home tomorrow."

Three days before Christmas Eve. Percy felt her lip tremble again and didn't trust herself to speak.

"Percy? Did I lose you?"

"No. I just...oh, Piers! That is wonderful news!"

"Is there any snow left? I'd like to take the boys tobogganing."

Percy glanced out the window where light flakes were falling, redeeming the boggy mud that the melted snow had

134

left from the week before. "We're getting some more as we speak. It should be perfect."

"Well, I have to run but I'll see you tomorrow." The line went quiet and she thought he had gone and waited for the beeps. "I've missed you, Percy."

"I've missed you too, darling."

After they hung up, she sat in the telephone chair, considering her emotions. Only an unfeeling brute could witness their friends being arrested for crimes against the government and murder, without it taking a toll. In some ways, she would never be the same. She suddenly felt delicate, fragile.

She had been proven right in most of her theories. But there was one part of the puzzle that she had missed. Bruce and Phoebe *had* been having an affair. It had not started off that way, but Phoebe had lost Walter to the booze and depression, as she had said, and Jemima had lost her youthful good looks, causing Bruce's eye to wander. When Percy considered those things, it was bound to happen. Phoebe and Bruce were both still young looking, vital and glamorous, and the thrill of the risky adventure just fueled the fire of attraction.

As she straightened some magazines on the telephone table, her thoughts drifted to the phone call she had received yesterday from Ellen Richmond. Mark had turned up at her mother's, safe and sound. The man who had drowned was one of the muscle men sent to rough him up. He had pulled Mark's wallet out of his jacket to taunt him and slipped it into his own pocket, before knocking Mark around. As they tussled, the thug had fallen into the river and Mark had not waited around to see if he survived. In a split second, he decided it was high time to go underground.

When Mark finally made contact with Ellen, she had convinced him that surviving day to day in the shadows was no way to live and that the children deserved better. He had gone to the police and pleaded guilty to receiving stolen goods and would serve some time in prison.

Percy ambled into the living room and looked out the window, smiling as she watched the boys trying to make snowballs. It was not going very well but judging by the delighted expressions on their faces, it didn't matter. Plumping the cushions on the settee, Percy's mind wandered to the Howards. During the course of Inspector Brown's investigation, it was discovered that Tom had been involved in embezzling funds from his accounting clients. Since their expenses had outstripped their income for some years and the historic house they lived in had needed improvements that had cost a pretty penny, they were chronically short of cash. The embezzlement was about to be uncovered at his company, which accounted for his somber mood during the party. At any moment, the axe would drop.

In a surprising twist, Verity had declared that she would stand by her man, renouncing the gardener and promising to support Tom through whatever punishment was handed down.

A sudden squeal caught Percy's attention. The boys had started throwing the snowballs at each other. How she would miss them when they went back to school. Perhaps when Piers heard how she had discovered the cook's body and that she had been instrumental in bringing the traitors to justice, he might reconsider her views on boarding school.

Well, it was worth a try.

The End

Thanks for buying my book!

Ann Sutton

I hope you enjoyed, *Death at a Christmas Party,* and love Percy as much as I do. This is book 1 of my new series, *Percy Pontefract Mysteries.*

I also write another cozy mystery series, The Dodo Dorchester Mystery series. If you are interested in a **free** prequel to that series go to https://dl.bookfunnel.com/997vvive24 and download *Mystery at the Derby.*

For more information about the series go to my website at www.annsuttonauthor.com and subscribe to my newsletter.

You can also follow me on Facebook at: https://www.facebook.com/annsuttonauthor

About the Author

Agatha Christie plunged Ann Sutton into the fabulous world of reading when she was 10. She was never the same. She read every one of Christie's books she could lay her hands on. Mysteries remain her favorite genre to this day - so it was only natural that she would eventually write my own.

Born and raised in England, Ann graduated college with a double honors in Education and French. During her year abroad teaching English in France, she met her Californian husband. Married in London, they moved to California after her graduation.

Together with their growing family they bounced all around the United States, finally settling in the foothills of the Rocky Mountains.

After dabbling with writing over the years, Ann finally began in earnest when her youngest was in middle school. Covid lockdown pushed her to take her writing even more seriously and so was born the best-selling Dodo Dorchester Mystery Series. To date over 100, 000 units have been sold or read on KU.

You can find out more about Ann Sutton at annsuttonsuthor.com.

Acknowledgements

I would like to thank all those who have read my books, write reviews and provide suggestions as you continue to inspire.

I would also like to thank my critique partners, Laurie Snow Turner, Mary Malcarne Thomas and Lisa McKendrick

So many critique groups are overly critical. I have found with you guys a happy medium of encouragement, cheerleading and constructive suggestions. Thank you.

My proof-reader – Tami Stewart

The mothers of a large and growing families who read like the wind with an eagle eye. Thank you for finding little errors that have been missed.

My editor – Jolene Perry of Waypoint Author Academy

Sending my work to editors is the most terrifying part of the process for me but Jolene offers correction and constructive criticism without crushing my fragile ego.

My cheerleader, marketer and IT guy – Todd Matern

A lot of the time during the marketing side of being an author I am running around with my hair on fire. Todd is the yin to my yang. He calms me down and takes over when I am yelling at the computer.

My beta readers – Francesca Matern, Stina Van Cott,

Your reactions to my characters and plot are invaluable.

The Writing Gals for their FB author community and their YouTube tutorials

These ladies give so much of their time to teaching their Indie author followers how to succeed in this brave new publishing world. Thank you.

Printed in Great Britain
by Amazon